Dear Reader

From my first childh... Scotland and her peo... is especially beautiful. I am also ... dynamics of small communities, and the special people who provide dedicated health care in these areas, developing a broad interest in their patients and wider families. So I was determined to write what will be three linked books within this setting.

If you were kind enough to read my first Mills & Boon® Medical Romance™, THE ITALIAN DOCTOR'S BRIDE, you will have met Dr Hannah Frost and Italian locum Dr Nic di Angelis. They make a guest appearance in this, my second Medical Romance™, A DOCTOR WORTH WAITING FOR, which tells the story of Dr Conor Anderson, irreverent, caring and drop-dead gorgeous, and Dr Kate Fisher, a woman guarding secrets and inner pain.

Coming to work in sleepy Glentown-on-Firth, Kate has not counted on meeting someone like Conor. Can the breathtaking landscape, close-knit community and Conor's care combine to help Kate face her past? Conor and Kate are very special to me, and I hope you will enjoy their book. Look out for mentions of Kyle Sinclair and Alexandra Patterson—I hope to tell their story very soon!

Happy reading

Margaret McDonagh

TOP-NOTCH DOCS

He's not just the boss, he's the best there is!

These heroes aren't just doctors, they're life-savers.

These heroes aren't just surgeons, they're skilled masters. Their talent and reputation are admired by all.

These heroes are devoted to their patients.
They'll hold the littlest babies in their arms, and melt the hearts of all who see.

These heroes aren't just medical professionals.
They're the men of your dreams.

A DOCTOR WORTH WAITING FOR

BY
MARGARET McDONAGH

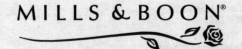

MILLS & BOON®

All the characters in this book have no existence outside the imagination of the author, and have no relation whatsoever to anyone bearing the same name or names. They are not even distantly inspired by any individual known or unknown to the author, and all the incidents are pure invention.

First published in Great Britain 2007
Paperback edition 2007
Harlequin Mills & Boon Limited,
Eton House, 18-24 Paradise Road, Richmond, Surrey TW9 1SR

© Margaret McDonagh 2007

ISBN-13: 978 0 263 85228 8
ISBN-10:   0 263 85228 8

Set in Times Roman 10½ on 13¼ pt
03-0307-57371

Printed and bound in Spain
by Litografia Rosés, S.A., Barcelona

Margaret McDonagh says of herself: 'I began losing myself in the magical world of books from a very young age, and I always knew that I had to write, pursuing the dream for over twenty years, often with cussed stubbornness in the face of rejection letters! Despite having numerous romance novellas, short stories and serials published, the news that my first "proper book" had been accepted by Harlequin Mills & Boon® for their Medical Romance™ line brought indescribable joy! Having a passion for learning makes researching an involving pleasure, and I love developing new characters, getting to know them, setting them challenges to overcome. The hardest part is saying goodbye to them, because they become so real to me. And I always fall in love with my heroes! Writing and reading books, keeping in touch with friends, watching sport and meeting the demands of my four-legged companions keeps me well occupied. I hope you enjoy reading this book as much as I loved writing it.'

You can contact Margaret at
http://margaretmcdonagh.bravehost.com

Recent titles by the same author:

THE ITALIAN DOCTOR'S BRIDE

With thanks to Gwen Baxter, Michael Quigley,
Lucy Hadley of the Forestry Commission,
Scottish Ambulance Service and Galloway
Mountain Rescue for generous research advice.

And to Gill, Gwen, Wolfie, The Grumpies and
my Guardian Angels, without whom
I would cease to function.

CHAPTER ONE

'HAVE you heard the news? Did Fred reach you?'

'I have and he did.' Dr Conor Anderson smiled at Aileen Nichol, their first-rate practice manager, whose question greeted him as he arrived at the surgery on Tuesday morning. 'I was out hillwalking with Kyle Sinclair,' he continued, referring to his best friend, a fellow GP who worked out of the Rigtownbrae practice some miles away. Arriving home late, he had found a message from his partner, Fred Murdoch. 'I gather our new locum has arrived early.'

Aileen nodded with customary vigour, her dark red curls bobbing. 'Yesterday.'

Kate Fisher had been recommended by Fred's old friend, Professor James Fielding-Smythe, a renowned London-based surgeon. Rather than the traditional interview, her CV had been faxed through and Fred had spoken with her and James at length by telephone. There was no doubt Kate's qualifications and references were impressive but Conor was intrigued by the gaps. He had not noticed them at first, they were well hidden—intentionally or not he had yet to discover—but there were unexplained breaks between recent employment dates. Why? And why did Kate, highly qualified and used to a busy London practice, want to locum in rural south-west Scotland? She would have her pick of jobs.

Fred was anxious to give Kate a chance and, despite his reservations, Conor had backed his older partner's judgement. The niggling feeling remained that Fred knew more than he'd let on, which increased Conor's curiosity. But he trusted Fred. And Fred trusted James, whose endorsement of Kate was glowing. Why one of Europe's top orthopaedic specialists should involve himself in the career moves of a young GP was another puzzle Conor had yet to solve.

'What's Kate like?' he asked, propping his medical bag on top of the reception counter.

'She's a lovely lassie, but…' The expression in Aileen's grey eyes turned thoughtful as she paused and his attention sharpened. 'I don't know how to explain it, Conor. She's guarded. I sensed…something.' She shrugged and frowned at him. 'Fred's protective of her.'

That had been his impression, too. Fred had been cagey on the phone, giving scant information about the new doctor. 'Do you know why, Aileen?'

'No. He took her to lunch before house calls. I introduced her to the others, then took her upstairs to the flat. Kate seemed nervous at the interest in her, uneasy answering questions about herself.'

'It's daunting meeting a group of strangers, especially a nosy lot like you!' Conor teased, although Kate's reaction was interesting.

Aileen swatted his arm in affectionate reprimand. 'Get away with you.'

'Any reason why Kate arrived earlier than arranged?'

'She knew her predecessor left last week and suspected we'd be pleased for her to start,' the older woman explained.

'That sounds reasonable. We can certainly use the help. Let's hope she continues to be as conscientious.'

'I can't imagine Kate being unreliable,' Aileen commented, setting out his tray of patient notes for morning surgery.

Conor hoped not. Would the city girl find herself a fish out of water in sleepy but beautiful Glentown-on-Firth? The secrecy surrounding Kate, the gaps in her CV and Aileen's impressions sparked his curiosity.

'With Fred at the care trust meeting, we decided Kate should sit in on my consultations and house calls,' he informed Aileen, picking up his medical bag and wedging the tray of notes under his arm.

'I doubt you'll find that a hardship.' Aileen smiled, her eyes mischievous.

'Yeah?' Conor raised a speculative eyebrow. 'If Kate's as good a doctor as we've been led to believe, I'll be happy. Will you let me know when she comes in, please?'

'She's here.'

Aileen's pronouncement had him turning back in surprise. 'She is? Where?'

'She's waiting for you in the private sitting room. I thought it would be quieter for you to introduce yourselves there than in the bustle of the staffroom.'

'Thanks, Aileen.' Grateful for her thoughtfulness, his smile was warm. 'I'll go and collect her. Give us a few moments to get acquainted before sending anyone through.'

'Of course. Buzz when you're ready. I'll update Jenny,' she added, as the young receptionist arrived for work. As he went to move away, Aileen rested her hand on his arm. 'Conor, be careful with Kate.'

As he headed through the rambling old building to his consulting room, Aileen's words preyed on his mind. What was it about Kate that inspired concern in people? The professor, Fred…now Aileen. Soon he could form his own opinion. A ripple of anticipation shivered down his spine, catching him unawares. Leaving his things in his room, he headed along the corridor, pausing at the staffroom to say good morning before continuing to the cosy sitting room they used for various situations from breaking bad news to distressed patients to providing a quiet space should a member of staff need privacy.

He paused at the doorway, his appreciative gaze locked on the sole occupant of the room. The woman was stunning. He had been intrigued to meet Kate Fisher but had never imagined that his first sight of her would send his senses whirling and set his heart thudding. Tense, she stood by the window, her arms folded across her chest, even white teeth worrying the sensual curve of her lower lip. His breath caught. Glossy brown hair, the colour of polished walnut, fell to her shoulders in a satiny curtain. Her face was captivating, her smooth complexion olive-toned, the bare minimum of make-up enhancing her natural beauty. She had perfect cheekbones, slightly slanting eyes, straight nose and that sensual, irresistible mouth with luscious, dusky-rose lips he found himself longing to taste.

She looked younger than her thirty-two years. Above average height, she was dressed in a charcoal-grey trouser suit that hinted at the deliciously curvy figure beneath. Red-hot desire slammed inside him. He shook his head to clear the fog that hazed his brain, shocked by his instinctive response to this woman.

Walking towards her, he saw a pallor underlying her skin, making him wonder if she had been ill, and then he met her gaze and all other thoughts faded. She had the saddest eyes he had ever seen. Dark brown, fringed with long lashes, they were soulful, full of hurt and loss. There was pain here, some terrible inner torment she was struggling to conceal or avoid, and in that moment he determined he was going to discover what was troubling her and do something about it. The urge to hold her, comfort her, protect her was as overwhelming as the fresh wave of desire that coursed through him, more intense than anything he had ever experienced.

Kate stared in shock at the man who entered the room, taken aback by his striking good looks, the dark blond hair, short at the back and sides but thick and wayward on top, falling in unruly fashion across his forehead. In his mid-thirties, around six feet tall, his athletic frame was dressed in the kind of leg-hugging jeans that ought to be illegal and a long-sleeved white T-shirt that suggested at the leanly muscled definition of his chest, arms and shoulders. Smooth-shaven, his jaw was masculine without being heavy, his cheeks lean, his nose in perfect proportion to his other features, and his mouth, curved now in a small but sinful smile, was temptingly kissable. He was the most gorgeous, intensely sexy man she had ever seen. Startled, her gaze clashed with his, the warmth and obvious interest in his riveting green eyes enough to suck every scrap of air from her lungs.

'Hello, Kate.' The husky, gently accented voice was impossibly intimate, wrapping around her, ensnaring her. She battled the instinctive urge to back away as he breached the gap between them, his body close enough that she could scent his earthy male aroma. 'I'm Conor Anderson.'

'You are?'

Unable to mask her surprise, cursing her inane reply, Kate could do nothing but stare, swallowing against the lump lodging in her throat as she assessed his casual clothes, his heart-stopping appeal. He didn't look like any doctor she had ever seen. Oh, hell! Coming here was meant to be safe. But there was nothing safe about this man, or the way her blood was singing in her veins as an unwanted curl of desire knotted her insides. No! She didn't want this. She had come here to sort out her professional life, not complicate things further. She didn't need the warning bells clanging in her brain to know that Conor Anderson was someone to steer clear of. The comments of the staff the previous afternoon had alerted her…Conor was a womaniser and a serial heartbreaker.

Conor has quite a reputation across the county.
You won't have worked with anyone like our Conor before!

You're going to love him, Kate. Everyone loves Conor.
Especially the women!

And he loves them—providing they don't expect too much
or try to hold him.

The trail of disappointed women left in his wake will testify
he's a perpetual bachelor.

It doesn't stop them making a play for him, though. Men
like Conor don't come along very often. He's enough to make
many a woman think it worth the risk of breaking her heart.

The laughing remarks flashed through her mind and she
recalled the brief asides Fred Murdoch had made during their
telephone conversations before she had accepted the locum
position. Fred had joked about Conor not yet settling down
and always finding himself the centre of attention. Female attention. She should have given more credence to her uneasi-
ness at those words at the time but she had been too nervous
about the job to pay proper attention to her early-warning
system. Ignoring that flicker of unease had been a mistake.
Now, as she assessed Conor, she was paying the price for her
lapse. He looked more like someone from a bad girl's erotic
dream than a professional doctor, she decided with unease
and disapproval. Focusing back on his face, she discovered
him studying her, amusement shining in those green eyes.

'Welcome to Glentown-on-Firth.'

'Thank you.'

He held out his hand but the last thing she wanted was to
touch him, scared what might happen if she did. Had James
Fielding-Smythe had done this on purpose? He had been
evasive about Conor Anderson when persuading her to take
this post, focusing on the older, unthreatening Fred Murdoch
and sidestepping her queries about the younger partner. But
the prof would know how this full-of-himself doctor with a
womanising reputation would affect her and she had made
another miscalculation by allowing James to distract her attention. Conor made her think of Darren, pain and humilia-

tion. Things that were two years in the past, pushed to the back of her mind by the far worse events that had happened since then to challenge her. But she remembered. And it was not a place she planned to revisit, no matter how outwardly appealing the man and how strong the temptation.

The unwanted frisson of awareness that rippled through her when she forced herself to complete the handshake, as politeness dictated, was worse than she'd anticipated. His fingers curled around hers, firm and warm, holding her longer than convention demanded, his touch sending a lightning bolt of sensation shooting up her arm and searing along her nerve endings with the force of a million watts. She knew Conor felt it too because his eyes darkened and his lips parted, mirroring her own involuntary response. Alarmed, she snatched her hand free, unable to meet that intense green gaze, stepping back, desperate to put space between them. But the distance did nothing to lessen his impact. She could feel his touch, scent his earthy fragrance, an inappropriate flare of arousal burning inside her. The knowledge that she would have to spend time with him while she learned her way around the area filled her with dismay. She needed to keep as far from him as possible. Conor Anderson was dangerous.

'We're pleased you chose to join us, Kate.' The warm intimacy of his voice sent a fresh shiver down her spine. 'What made you decide to come to Scotland?'

'The job was highly recommended,' she explained, tensing as she worried what other questions he might have.

'Your qualifications are impressive—we're lucky to have you.'

She didn't know about that. At the professor's instigation, she had reworked her CV, hoping neither GP partner would notice that the information was not one hundred per cent comprehensive. She had tried to disguise any gaps but had deliberately omitted mention of her additional surgical skills and the advanced trauma life support course. Neither had she mentioned the work she had done this past year. The last thing she wanted was to explain where she had been and why she had given it up. It was in the past and she planned it would stay that way. There was no need for anyone to know. It had no bearing on the present—except in her own head, feeding her doubts and bringing her nightmares.

'There won't be much call for your expertise in tropical medicine here.' Kate smothered a groan at Conor's remark, realising she had concentrated on searching for surgical references and had forgotten to remove the tropical diseases and hygiene diploma. 'An interesting line of study.'

'The opportunity was there and it was another string to my bow.'

Kate's heart sank. Conor had obviously considered her CV with more care than Fred had. Hoping Conor would be satisfied, having no wish to impart further information, she flicked him a glance, her tension increasing as he watched her with silent interest.

'I expect the situation in London is very different,' he said after a long pause, his smile implying he knew there was more behind her answer but deciding, much to her relief, to let her off the hook. For now.

'I've seen several malaria cases in practice there, plus a couple of more unusual diseases.'

Leaning against the sofa, Conor regarded her, his green eyes steady. 'I know you talked with Fred yesterday and I believe he explained our routines and back-up staff. Aside from general surgeries and home visits, I'm responsible for the diabetic clinic and the diet and fitness group, while Fred holds the ante—and postnatal clinics. The mother and baby group is covered by us both. We share other things like the stopping-smoking, well-woman, male-health clinics and so on. And minor surgery.' His gaze turned speculative. 'I understand the latter doesn't interest you.'

'No.' Kate fought the sickness in her stomach. The prof

might think she was capable but she had lost her nerve for surgery. What scared her was whether she had lost her nerve to be any kind of doctor. 'I don't do surgery.'

Her response had been stiff and she could feel Conor looking at her, knew he had questions. She held her breath, releasing it when he finally moved on. 'We only handle minor procedures—Fred and I will cover those. Dorothy Scott, our nurse practitioner, deals with any small injuries, so you won't be faced with anything but the odd bit of stitching in an emergency. Would that be all right?'

'Yes, of course.'

'Ease yourself in at your own pace, Kate, and always ask if there is anything you want to know.' That unsettling gaze focused on her again. 'We want your stay to be a happy one.'

All she wanted was to keep her head down but she nodded all the same. 'I understand there won't be out-of-hours work?'

'No.' Conor shifted, folding his arms across his chest, a frown on his face. 'We signed on for cover when the new system came in. Fred was finding the long hours increasingly tiring. I— Well, never mind. We rotate Saturday morning surgery between us, so you'll only do one in three. Saturday is for emergency drop-ins, rather than appointments. You won't be asked to work evenings or Sundays.'

Not that she would mind. She preferred maintaining involvement with patients but the current working arrangements were widely adopted and she could understand an older man like Fred choosing to slow down. What had Conor been going to say about himself before he'd thought better of it? No doubt he valued the extra time to devote to his hectic social life.

'Have you settled in upstairs?'

She swallowed as Conor squeezed his hands into the pockets of his jeans, tightening the fabric across his hips, drawing her attention back to his body. 'The flat is very comfortable, thank you.'

'I hope you won't find Glentown too quiet after the city life you are used to.'

The doubt in his voice made her wonder if Conor had less confidence in her position here than Fred did. 'I'm sure I won't.'

Far from it, if only he knew. The quiet life, rural location and the solitude of walking in the hills were major draws of this job. Peace and space were what she needed to regroup, restore her shattered spirit and think about the rest of her life.

'Let us know if there is anything you need or anything we can do to for you while you are here.'

'I will.' He meant the flat, the job, she reminded herself, trying not to react to the husky suggestiveness of his voice. 'Everything is fine.'

Everything except Conor himself—and the fact that she was scared witless about her adequacy as a doctor. Why had she let her father and the professor talk her into taking this post? It was easy for them to tell her it was time to move on but she felt she had failed, was unsure she had anything left to give.

A fresh wave of panic welled inside her and she curled her hands into fists, battling the overwhelming urge to run—to run from facing a challenge that felt too big, too soon, too scary. Helplessly, she looked at Conor. His clear eyes watched her and she could see curiosity mix with a warm compassion that caused an uncharacteristic threat of tears. Blinking them away, she started as he reached out and took her hand, his fingers giving hers a reassuring squeeze.

'First days are always difficult.'

Kate shrugged, not trusting herself to speak, frightened she would do the unthinkable and blurt everything out, confide in him, explain this wasn't first-day nerves. What was it about this man that got inside her skin? But she couldn't forget his reputation, how very wrong he would be for her, or why she was here and what she had to do to get her life back on track and mend her battered soul.

* * *

Conor wasn't sure what had happened but he was positive Kate had been on the verge of confiding something before there had been an emotional withdrawal and a shoring up of her defences. He sensed that whatever had caused that sudden welling of panic and anxiety was about more than new job unease. Now barriers were being placed between them, Kate's inner disquiet and wariness obvious. Something much deeper was going on here but it would take time and patience to gain her trust and break through her reserve—if he wanted to take things further. Which he did. More than anything. His innate concern for anyone or anything in pain meant he couldn't leave her hurting, but getting past her defences and persuading her there was something special here worth exploring wouldn't be easy.

Aware of her tension, he brushed the pad of his thumb across the back of her hand before he let her go and forced himself to give her space. He missed the contact, missed being close enough that the citrusy fragrance of her toyed with his senses, but he needed to keep things businesslike…for now.

'We have a busy morning and plenty of patients waiting. Do you feel ready to make a start?'

'OK.' Her eyes closed for a moment and when she opened them again he was struck by the thread of fear in the dark brown depths.

Concerned for her, he tried to ease the tension with humour. 'Don't worry, Kate, I don't bite. Not like that, anyway!'

His teasing comment backfired. All he could think about were the many parts of Kate he desperately yearned to taste and to nibble, the fire of desire reigniting inside him. Hell! He saw the flush tinge her cheeks before his gaze captured hers. The disapproval in her eyes amused and troubled him. He had diverted her from her fear but only at the expense of making her think he was some kind of lech, which was not what he had intended at all. Sighing, he led the way back to his consulting room, unable to get the sight, sound and scent of Kate Fisher out of his mind.

Instead of finding answers, meeting this woman had raised more questions. Everything about Kate intrigued him…and made him more certain than ever that she was hiding something, that there were secrets waiting to be unravelled.

CHAPTER TWO

KATE tried to wrench her gaze from the distraction of Conor's sublime rear view as she followed him along the wide, airy corridor. She had been unsettled by his throw-away comment. She was sure he hadn't meant anything sexual by it but all she could think about was what his mouth might taste like, how his lips and teeth would feel caressing her skin. This was appalling. It had to stop. Now. She was here to get her career back on track, to see if she could be a doctor after the traumatic events of the last months. It may have been too long since she had been held and loved, but now was not the time to start yearning for male companionship. And Conor was *not* the right man to turn to, not with his apparent legion of ladies and aversion to commitment. He confused her. She had been forewarned of his heartbreaker reputation, she disapproved of his womanising, the unprofessional, casual way he dressed and approached being a doctor, and yet he had displayed a sensitivity to her feelings she would never have expected. She took a seat in Conor's consulting room and tried to focus on the job ahead, nerves clenching in her stomach and making her feel sick, her doubts returning with a vengeance.

'All right?' Conor asked, taking the first packet of notes from the full tray on his desk.

Taking a deep breath, aware he again seemed attuned to

her mood, Kate nodded. 'Fine,' she lied, feeling the intensity of his regard before he reached for the phone.

'Hi, Jenny,' he said and Kate visualised the young receptionist with the long blonde hair who had been Conor's chief fan the previous afternoon. 'We're ready for Andrea now. Thanks, sweetie.'

'Andrea?' Kate queried as they waited, trying to ignore his throw-away endearments and the intimate familiarity in his voice when he spoke to women.

'Mmm.' He took the notes out of their folder. 'One of my ladies.'

'I see,' she murmured stiffly, unable to prevent her feelings showing in her tone.

'Do you?'

Kate's expression closed, her mouth tightening in disapproval. She had heard he was unorthodox but surely he wasn't so unprofessional that he had any kind of relationship with a patient? Glancing up, she saw the knowing expression in his green eyes, her breath catching when he flashed her a naughty grin before he stood up and walked towards the door.

'The very lady I've been longing to see.' Kate watched him smile at whoever was approaching along the corridor, his tone affectionate. 'Now I know why I make sure you're my first appointment in the morning. Gets my day off to a good start to see a beautiful woman. Come on in, Andrea.'

Steeling herself to be polite to some flirty bimbo, Kate struggled to prevent her mouth dropping open as Conor guided an older lady inside. She was clearly in pain, two walking sticks held with difficulty in her weakened hands. There was a quiet dignity in her thin face and pale blue eyes as Conor helped her across the room to a chair.

'Seems you've already found yourself a beautiful woman,' Andrea commented with a friendly smile, shifting around to find a more comfy position. 'Trust you, Conor!'

Kate was subjected to the full force of Conor's sultry green eyes. 'You're both beautiful. I'm a lucky man this morning. Andrea, say hello to our new doctor, Kate Fisher. Kate, Andrea Milne,' he introduced them, rounding his desk to sit down.

'I'm pleased to meet you,' Kate managed, trying to ignore the wild beat of her pulse after Conor's intense look, the exchange with Andrea adding fuel to the rumours about his reputation.

'You, too, dear. Good to see a fresh face…and such a pretty one.'

Kate noticed Conor smile before he glanced at Andrea's notes then returned his full attention to his patient. 'How is my favourite lady today?'

'Better for seeing you.' Andrea chuckled, colour washing her pale cheeks. 'I wish I was thirty again, not sixty!'

Conor winked at her, his smile teasing. 'Me, too.'

Kate waited while Conor chatted about Andrea's symptoms, watching as he knelt on the floor to conduct a gentle examination of the lady's troublesome hands and feet. There were signs of subluxation of the wrist, along with muscle wastage and the beginnings of deformity in the hands. She feared Andrea might go on to develop the classic swan-neck shape to the fingers typical of rheumatoid arthritis.

'Any more trouble with your knee?' Conor's question was casual but Kate could see the care with which he checked the joint and listened to the reply.

'Some twinges, but nothing like before,' Andrea explained.

'And your wrists?'

'The splints you recommended have been a real help.'

Conor sat back on his heels, pushing a wayward fall of hair back from his forehead as he smiled. 'Good. We'll keep a close eye on the knee. If it flares up again we can consider an injection of steroids into the joint to help the problem. How's your other pain, Andrea? Any problems?'

'I'm coping, dear,' she allowed with a brave smile.

'We want to do our best for you.' Kate's breath caught as Conor turned to her. 'We caught Andrea's condition early when she began having problems. The deterioration has been gradual, with a few more acute relapses from time to time. We referred her to the rheumatologist and started disease-modifying drugs,' he explained, and Kate nodded, knowing the DMARDs worked slowly over months to gain their effect, hopefully slowing the progression of the disease and aiding stiffness and inflammation. 'Andrea has been settled on me-thotrexate for a while now, which was combined with a low-dose steroid. We do regular checks on her blood pressure and symptom progression, plus the usual bloods, biochemistry and so on every three months.' He paused again to smile at Andrea, resting a hand on her forearm. 'You've not had any side-effects or new symptoms?'

'No, dear. Just the usual stiffness and discomfort.'

Conor frowned with concern. 'Andrea's had reduced appetite, tiredness and a loss of grip and mobility, but we try to balance a programme of medication to help manage her pain and use a team approach with the nurses and our visiting physiotherapist involved in keeping her as mobile as possible.'

'And wonderful you all are,' Andrea praised, her gratitude evident, along with her fondness for Conor.

Kate felt chastened at the way she had judged Conor's aptitude as a doctor. She had expected a self-interested romeo, if not playing at being a doctor then certainly not taking the job seriously. She had never imagined he would care this much. True, he dripped sex appeal from every pore, but behind the casual clothes, irreverent humour and wicked smile was a watchful, concerned doctor who worked to put people at their ease, valuing the whole person. And he took his time. If all his consultations were like this, they were in for a long day, but she didn't mind because patient care was her top priority, too. She had been wrong about his professional skills, but although she could learn a lot from this man she knew it was a bad idea to spend more time than necessary in his company.

After Conor has escorted Andrea along to Dorothy, the nurse practitioner, who would take care of the blood tests, he returned to the room and called for their next patient, a middle-aged man with breathing problems. Kate soon discovered Conor was as caring and irreverent with his male patients as his female ones.

'We've had the X-rays back, Jim. I'm glad to say that there are no signs of growths or tumours.'

The man's relief was palpable. 'Thank goodness for that' He tried to laugh but stopped short, wheezing uncomfortably.

'You do have a nasty infection and some fluid on the lungs,' Conor continued, listening to Jim's chest and taking his blood pressure. 'I'm going to prescribe some new medication and I want you to come back and see me next week—call me sooner if you don't notice any improvement or you are worried, OK?'

'Sure, Doc. Thanks.'

Conor tapped some instructions on his keyboard then signed the prescription form that emerged from the printer, handing it over with a rueful smile. 'I suppose you haven't stopped smoking, Jim?'

'Well…' The man looked sheepish. 'I am trying, Doc but it's not easy to give up. I've smoked since I was fourteen. I know it's naughty but I enjoy it.'

'Many naughty activities are pleasurable,' Conor murmured as he rose to his feet, and Kate willed herself not to blush when he glanced at her with a cheeky smile, leaving her in no doubt what he was thinking. 'In your case, though, Jim, smoking is damaging your health. I know it's difficult, but do the best you can. If there's anything I can do, referring you or trying patches, come and talk to me.'

'I will, Doc. Thank you. Good to meet you, lass,' Jim added, as Conor showed him from the room.

Kate kept her eyes averted when Conor returned to his desk. She was struggling with his wicked aside, her mind disobeying her as she imagined in vivid detail far too many sinfully pleasurable and very naughty things she was sure Conor would be all too expert at doing.

Heat flared inside her but she fought to ignore the unwanted desire. No way was she going there. Especially with him. She had too many issues to face while she was here without allowing herself to become one of the bevy of women Conor was rumoured to juggle in his life and adding another notch to his legendary bedpost.

Her head knew all that...she just hoped the rest of her body would behave.

'How about taking the next consultation yourself?' Conor suggested, watching the play of emotions across Kate's face.

She had been annoyed with him earlier and he had known straight away that she had misinterpreted his comments about Andrea. It troubled him that Kate could imagine he behaved improperly with patients. Was it just him or had something happened that made her view male doctors with disdain and distrust? He hadn't been able to resist teasing her. Keeping her off balance, combined with her genuine interest in the consultations, had banished her alarm, but now that he had suggested she take the next patient, the anxiety and flash of fear were back in those far-too-serious brown eyes.

'Sure.'

She wouldn't look at him and he sensed the veneer of outward assurance was wafer-thin. Kate had a crisis of confidence. He had no idea why. Not yet. But he'd find out. 'Our next patient is Julie MacIntyre. She's 23 and a first-time mother. Her son Dominic is three months old.'

'Any idea why she's coming in today?'

'No.' He swallowed as Kate flicked strands of satiny hair behind her shoulder, exposing the curve of her neck. His heart started thudding again and he cursed under his breath. He had to stop looking at her and concentrate on the job. Thankful when Julie arrived, he rose to his feet, sweeping Dominic out of the young woman's arms to hug him, something else that surprised Kate, he noticed. 'Goodness, haven't you grown, young man?'

'He gets heavier by the day.' Julie laughed.

'Julie, meet our new doctor, Kate Fisher,' Conor said, balancing chubby little Dominic against his chest, immediately understanding why Julie had brought her son to see them. 'If it's all right with you, Kate will take your consultation today.'

'That's fine.' The young woman smiled. 'Hello, Dr Fisher.'

'Kate, please.'

Relieved at the friendly opening, Conor realised he had yet to see Kate smile. As he relinquished Dominic back to Julie and returned to his chair, he watched Kate nervously begin the consultation, determined that his goal for the first week was to make her smile. Somehow. Even once.

'What can we do for you today, Julie?' Kate asked.

'I'm really worried about Dominic's eye,' the young woman explained, her anxiety obvious. 'I thought I should bring him right away.'

'You did the best thing. That's what we're here for,' Kate reassured her, as she moved round the desk, asking Julie more questions while she focused on the baby. 'Has Dominic ever had this problem before?'

'No, there's been no trouble with his eyes at all,' Julie confirmed.

'I'll take a swab to be on the safe side,' Kate explained, following Connor's directions to fetch what she needed, 'but I'm pretty sure it's a blocked tear duct. It's what we call sticky eye and it's not uncommon. Usually the passage hollows out around the time the baby is born but sometimes this can be delayed and become blocked. It's a problem that normally rights itself by the time the baby is a year or so old.

Dominic's eye doesn't look infected, so I won't be prescribing antibiotic drops just yet.'

Impressed, Conor sat back and let her get on with the job, enjoying watching the graceful way she moved, her ease with the baby, her gentleness and the thoughtful way she explained things to Julie. Whatever panic Kate had experienced before the consultation had begun had vanished once she had got into her stride, though he was still interested to know its cause.

'What will happen?' Julie asked, jigging the happy baby on her knee once Kate had finished taking the swab with gentle care.

'The best thing is for you to bathe his eye with boiled water to remove any debris. Make sure your hands are clean and keep the water comfortably warm. You can do it several times a day, perhaps when you have Dominic down to change his nappy.'

Julie let out a sigh of relief. 'Is that all?'

'It should clear up on its own,' Kate reassured her, almost managing a smile, Conor noted. 'Come back any time if you are worried. We'll see Dominic again in a few days to check how things are, and I'll let you know when we have the results of the swab—but I'm pretty sure it is a blocked duct.'

'Thank you so much.'

'No problem.'

When Kate moved to see them out, Julie hesitated, grinning as she held Dominic out to Connor for a final cuddle, and Conor smiled, brushing a finger down one warm, pudgy cheek. 'Take care, young man. You, too, Julie.'

'We will. Bye, Conor. Thanks again.'

As Kate returned to the desk, he waited for her to complete the necessary paperwork for the swab and make up the notes. 'Nicely done, Kate.'

She murmured an acknowledgement, appearing embarrassed by his praise, still not meeting his gaze. He was impatient to find out more about her but there was no time to waste as their next patient arrived.

Conor made sure Kate took various cases for the rest of morning surgery, satisfied as time went by that they had an exceptionally good doctor in their midst. Whether she believed in herself was another matter. When their list was over, they snatched a few moments for a hasty drink before house calls and he discovered Kate shared his taste for hot chocolate. Other staff were on a break and he noted Kate's wariness if anyone asked a direct question about her life or her work.

She was tense when they left the surgery but by the time they had completed most of the visits on the list and were in the car heading back towards Glentown-on-Firth for their final call, Conor was even more impressed with her work. She established a rapport with patients, and he was delighted with her kindness, her ability to listen and the way she treated everyone with genuine respect and patience. Although she still hadn't smiled. Nothing more than a tilt of her lips that failed to strip the deep inner sadness from her eyes.

'This is a beautiful area.'

Startled that she had initiated a conversation, he flicked her a glance before returning his attention to the narrow country road.

'It's wonderful. So are the people. I came here nine years ago and can't imagine ever living anywhere else,' he told her, keen to keep her talking, hoping to change the poor opinion she had formed of him. 'It's a diverse region with many varied environments.'

'You don't come from around here?'

His childhood had not been stable or happy but that wasn't something he wanted to talk about. 'No. I trained in Aberdeen—that's where I met Kyle Sinclair, one of the GPs at the practice in Rigtownbrae. We both wanted to work in a rural area and were lucky to settle near each other. I love the hills, the outdoors. I have the best of both worlds in Glentown, the natural environment plus the satisfaction of community medicine, getting to know the patients and their families, being involved in their lives.'

'It must be rewarding,' she allowed, a wistful note in her voice.

'To me it is.' He glanced at her again, wishing he could get inside her head, know what she was thinking and feeling. 'Maybe you'll find it so, too.'

A sigh whispered from her lips. 'Maybe I will.'

'I know from your CV that you trained in London,' he probed, recalling the recent employment gaps that puzzled him. 'Has it always been the City for you?'

'Yes.'

The reply was clipped, her voice stiff, and he knew she was lying. As he slowed the car at a crossroads, he looked at her but she turned her head away. Her hands betrayed her, though. They were clasped in her lap, her knuckles white with tension. Driving on, he was convinced Kate's doubt and anxiety were deep-seated. This woman had secrets. Painful ones. His heart ached in response and he reached out a hand to cover hers, only to have her pull away from the contact, denying the comfort and understanding he yearned to offer.

'Kate, I—'

His was interrupted by the intrusion of his mobile phone and he cursed in frustration. As he searched for somewhere to pull off the narrow lane, Kate unwound her fingers and reached to take the phone from its rest.

'Shall I do it?'

'Thanks.'

'It's Jenny,' she told him after a moment, frowning as she listened. 'Yes, I'll tell him. Just a minute.'

'What is it?'

'Joyce Bingham has phoned to say that Lizzie Dalglish has fallen down the stairs. She's distressed and asking for you.'

New concern tightened in his chest. 'Tell Jenny we'll go

straight there, please, Kate, and ask her to ring Douglas, our next appointment, and tell him we'll be late.'

'OK.'

'And let Joyce know we'll be there soon.'

As Kate relayed the messages, Conor put his foot down, anxious about what they would find when they arrived.

CHAPTER THREE

'IS IT FAR?' Kate tightened her hold as Conor guided the four-wheel-drive with skill along the rural roads.

'About two miles. Joyce Bingham is Lizzie's next-door neighbour.'

The reply had been terse and she dared a glance at his set face. Lizzie was someone he cared about but, then, he had demonstrated time and again his dedication to his patients. The morning had been full of surprises, misjudgements and close shaves, and she felt mentally exhausted from the time spent with Conor, fighting to ignore the sexual tension that crackled between them and desperate to deflect his probing questions and not divulge more about herself.

Within minutes Conor drew up outside three old farm-workers' cottages and Kate followed in his wake as he grabbed his bag and hurried up the path to the middle house, where the front door stood ajar.

'Conor, thank goodness you're here,' an anxious, middle-aged woman greeted them.

Kate saw him smile and give the woman's shoulder a re-assuring squeeze. 'Hello, Joyce. What happened?'

'I heard this fearful crash,' the woman explained. 'I knew Billy was at work and Yvonne had gone shopping, so I rushed round. Poor Lizzie's in a state. I've called the ambulance but she was asking for you. She wanted to move but I told her to stay where she was until you came.'

'You did perfectly,' he praised, introducing Kate as they stepped from the porch into a small sitting room. 'Joyce, could you be an angel and track down Yvonne for me?'

'Yes, of course.'

The woman seemed relieved to have something to do. Kate followed Conor as he made his way to the foot of the stairs, finding the frail figure of an elderly lady lying there, her head propped on a pillow, a blanket covering her. She watched as Conor knelt down and took one thin, papery hand in his.

'Lizzie? Can you hear me?'

'Conor?' The thready voice was a mere whisper as pale blue eyes opened and struggled to focus.

'I'm here,' he soothed. 'What have you been doing to yourself?'

A grimace crossed the pain-ravaged face. 'So silly. Should have waited for Yvonne,' she confided, her voice a little stronger.

'Don't worry now. Did you trip on something? Can you remember? Did you feel dizzy or black out?'

'No, I wasn't dizzy. I caught my foot.'

'All right, Lizzie, we'll get you sorted out as quickly as we can,' Conor promised, reaching for his medical bag and turning back the blanket so he could check the elderly woman's condition and vital signs.

'Sorry to be such a nuisance.'

He tutted in disapproval. 'You're never a nuisance. Can you tell me where it hurts?'

'M-my right leg,' she managed, her face twisting with pain again.

Kate shifted to give Conor more room as he began to examine the woman's injuries. From where she stood, Kate could tell the femur was broken by the hip, the external rotation and shortening evident. Her gaze met Conor's as he glanced up with a grimace, sadness dulling his green eyes.

As he returned his attention to Lizzie, Kate stepped carefully round the other side and knelt down, ready to help if he needed anything, wriggling closer in the tight space between their patient and the wall. 'Hello, Lizzie, I'm Kate, the new locum. I'm helping Conor today.'

'Lucky Conor.'

Kate heard him chuckle at the spirited reply. 'Does anything else hurt, Lizzie? Did you hit your head when you fell?' Connor probed. Kate could see nasty bruises along the frail limbs.

'No. Just my leg.'

After checking Lizzie's eyes and the reaction of her pupils, Conor monitored heart, lungs and blood pressure again, hooking the stethoscope round his neck and recovering Lizzie with the blanket. 'How bad's the pain, Lizzie?'

'Grim,' she confirmed, sounding tired.

'We'll give you something for that now,' he promised, and Kate drew up some analgesia, handing him the syringe so he could check and administer it. For a moment he looked right at her, his expression so warmly intimate that she forgot how to breathe. 'Thanks, Kate.'

'No problem.'

She lowered her lashes and forced herself to focus on writing up notes of what they had done, drugs used and doses given—information that would be required by the paramedics and hospital doctor. Anything but look at or think about Conor.

'It should start to ease now, Lizzie,' he was saying, sitting back on his heels after another check of her vital signs and holding her hand again. 'The ambulance will be here soon.'

The woman shook her head. 'No! Conor, I don't want to go to hospital.'

'I know you don't, sweetie,' he said gently, his voice calm in response to Lizzie's distress. 'But there's nothing else for it, I'm afraid. You've broken your thigh bone right by the hip and it has to be X-rayed and properly seen to.'

Lizzie's eyes closed and she was silent for a few moments. 'I'm not going to be claiming that dance from you any time soon, then, am I?' she rallied with a weak smile.

Moved both by Lizzie's spirit and Conor's compassion, Kate watched as he brushed some thinning strands of white hair back from the pale face, his softly accented voice husky with affection. 'I'll save you one, I promise.'

'Conor?' Joyce called, returning to the room. 'The ambulance is pulling up. I've rung the Glentown post office and Jeanie Harris is searching the village for Yvonne.'

'Thanks, Joyce, you're a star.'

Conor concentrated on keeping Lizzie as calm as possible as the paramedics arrived and prepared to transfer the fragile lady to the ambulance, putting in an IV line to give her fluids and placing her on oxygen. Kate accompanied them outside, noting how Conor held Lizzie's hand until the last moment.

'We'll take good care of her, Conor,' one of the paramedics promised, closing the back doors of the ambulance.

'I know you will.' Conor smiled, handing over his hastily scribbled letter plus the notes Kate had already prepared. 'Thanks, guys.'

They watched as the ambulance left, Joyce coming to stand beside them. 'Poor old Lizzie,' she sighed.

'Thanks for your help, you were great,' Conor said. 'Are you OK? You've had a shock.'

'Nothing a strong cup of tea won't help. Would you both like one?'

Glancing at his watch, he shook his head. 'We'd better not, Joyce, but thank you. I need to tell Yvonne about her mum, then we have a call to make before we get back for afternoon surgery. Ring me if you need anything, all right?'

'I will. Thank you, Conor.'

After packing up the medical bag, they left the house in time to see another car arrive, a woman in her mid-forties scrambling out and hurrying up the path towards them, tears shimmering in her eyes. 'Oh, Conor, I've just heard! Is Ma going to be all right? I never thought she'd do anything like this. I was only going out for some essentials.'

'It's not your fault, Yvonne. Lizzie's in the best possible hands,' he reassured her, giving her a sympathetic hug. 'Are you going to be able to get to the hospital?'

'Yes, thank you, I rang Billy and he's coming home straight away. We'll go together,' she told him with a watery smile.

'Billy is Yvonne's husband, manager of the village bank,' Conor explained, introducing them. 'Call if I can help. I'll ring the hospital later and be in to visit Lizzie when I can.'

'Bless you, Conor. I'm so relieved you were here.'

'Your mum's a special lady, Yvonne.'

A special lady but a frail one, Kate thought, climbing back into the car. 'Do you think Lizzie will be all right?'

'I hope so.' He shrugged, but she could see the concern on his face. She'd only been working with him half a day but her misjudgement of him as a doctor had been glaring. He cared deeply about these people. 'Lizzie's long-term prognosis is worrying. You know as well as I do the high mortality and disability rates after these sorts of fractures in a person of her age. Her bones are fragile and she's become infirm and unsteady recently—that's why she left her own house in the village to move in with Yvonne and Billy. It's not an ideal situation for any of them.'

'The stairs can't help.'

'No, they don't. Lizzie has a bed-sitting room upstairs as the only bathroom facilities are up there. It means she's restricted. And she misses the village activity and her friends.'

He lapsed into silence, a frown on his face, and she suspected he was wondering about a solution...if and when Lizzie was well enough to come home.

The rest of the day was hectic with the completion of the home visits followed by clinics, consultations and a couple

of minor emergencies, but Kate welcomed the busy pace
because it gave her little time to worry about the job or fret
about Conor. It was well after six before she was ready to
leave, and when she discovered Conor was giving advice to
a patient on the telephone she took the opportunity to escape.
She nodded goodbye from the corridor, ignoring his gesture
for her to wait, slipping past his consulting-room door before
he could detain her and subject her to any more uncomfortable questions. She needed to recharge her mental batteries
before facing him again.

After saying goodnight to those members of staff yet to
head for home, she declined their offers to join them for a
meal or a drink at the village pub, needing to be alone to
assess her first day. She walked round the side of the building
and down the path, unlocked the door and went up the stairs
to the spacious two-bedroom flat that was her home in
Glentown-on-Firth.

The village nestled at the foot of a wooded valley, bounded
along the southern edge by the coastline of the Solway Firth,
while to the north lay farmland, woods and the stunning
Galloway hills. Situated in the heart of the village, the Solway
Medical Centre was housed in an impressive two-storey granite
building under a slate roof. Originally two residential villas,
they had been combined and renovated with a modern exten-
sion added at the rear during a recent expansion of the practice.

Having telephoned her father in London to reassure him she
had survived her first day, the sound of his voice and his concerned support making her homesick, she prepared a light meal
and sat at the large bay window in the living room, blind to the
magnificent views because her mind was buzzing with thoughts
and images—far too many of them featuring Conor Anderson.

She would never forget her first sight of him. Or the instant
wave of desire she had experienced, more powerful than
anything she had felt before, but she was not ready to think
about involvement with a man again. Not yet. And certainly

not with a casual romeo like Conor who appeared to have half the women of south-west Scotland at his beck and call, each hoping to be the one to tame him but getting a broken heart for her trouble. No, she had enough problems sorting out her career and deciding what to do with the rest of her life.

Today she had learned that Conor's care for his patients was genuine. If there was anything to be done to make life easier for Lizzie and her family, Kate had no doubt he would do it. She had been concerned about Conor's casualness but the patients loved his easygoing, touchy-feely approach to their care. He was a maverick, not at all what she was used to, but she respected him as a doctor. As a man he scared the hell out of her. She had never responded so intensely to someone. Her stay here was always going to be difficult professionally—the unwanted physical attraction to Conor made the weeks ahead even more alarming.

'How did things go today?'

Conor seated himself in Fred's kitchen and gratefully accepted the drink offered to him. 'Thanks. It went well. We had a busy day, routine for the most part, but I'm afraid that Lizzie Dalglish had a fall down the stairs and has broken her femur.'

'Oh, no.' Fred frowned, stirring a teaspoon of sugar into his steaming drink. 'Have you heard how she is?'

'I rang the hospital before I left the surgery. She's come through the operation which is a good start. We'll have to see how her rehabilitation goes. I'll visit when Lizzie is well enough.'

Fred ran the palm of one hand over his balding pate, a characteristic habit when he was anxious or lost in thought. 'How did Kate get on?'

'I was very impressed; she's an excellent doctor.' He paused, declining to mention his intense and immediate attraction to her. Meeting Fred's blue gaze, he watched the older man's expression. 'I'm not sure Kate knows it, though.'

'Why do you say that?'

'She was tense, nervous about her work—at least until she got started,' he explained, knowing Fred well enough to tell when he was being evasive.

Looking away, Fred shrugged. 'That's not unusual for first days.'

'It was more than that,' Conor persisted, puzzling over his unanswered questions and still miffed at the way Kate had sneaked home, denying him the chance to speak with her again. 'She's more than capable of holding her own consultations, but I'll keep taking her on house calls until she's better acquainted with the area.'

'Good. That's fine. But I don't want to rush her.'

Again Conor sensed that his partner was protecting Kate. But from what? Why? 'Do you know her history?'

'Kate's?' Fred parried, delaying a response when Conor nodded. 'Not much.'

Frustrated, Conor frowned and rested his arms on the table. 'So tell me what you do know.'

'I can't tell you any more than I already have, Conor.'

'Come on, Fred! I'm a partner here, too.'

'Yes, you are. But I can't break a confidence, you know that.' The older man sighed.

'Kate's confidence…or the professor's?'

Fred's blue eyes were troubled. 'Both, I suppose. Kate hasn't spoken to me—and she doesn't know James has told me more than he said he would,' he admitted, clearly uncomfortable with the situation.

'But—'

'All we need to know is that Kate's not incompetent or in any kind of trouble.'

'I never thought she was incompetent.'

Conor's frowned deepened. He could never imagine Kate doing anything wrong, let alone being negligent. After her initial hesitancy he had seen how natural and thorough and caring she was, but she was definitely in trouble, if not professionally then in some other part of her life. He knew it. What he didn't know was the nature of the problem. Yet. With or without Fred's help, though, he intended to find out.

'Has Kate been ill?' he asked, remembering his initial concern about her pallor.

'She's a good doctor, Conor,' Fred insisted. 'Better than good. We are lucky to have her.'

'I know that.'

'She needs some time.'

Which told him precisely nothing. 'But—'

'If Kate wants to talk, she will. Stop pushing, OK?'

Conor wasn't satisfied that it was OK. Kate was hurting. Anyone could see that. And it wasn't in his nature to stand by and do nothing.

'Leave her alone, Conor.' Fred's voice was uncharacteristically stern. 'Kate's not someone for you to play with.'

Irritated, Conor rose to his feet. 'I'm not playing, Fred. Far from it.'

'Then give the woman some space.'

Kate was soon taking her own surgeries and settled into the new routine, grateful for the friendliness of staff and patients. Sometimes she struggled with an accent or unfamiliar phrase but misunderstandings were laughingly overcome. If only the minor incidents with language were her only problem. Even though Fred was back, she still found herself accompanying Conor on home visits and, much to her chagrin, it was becoming harder to maintain her resolve and her resistance. She tried to avoid him but he seemed intent on hanging around, driving her to distraction. She was novelty value, she reassured herself. It would soon wear off. What about his busy social life? How did he fit all the women in when he seemed to work such long hours? It was none of her business. Thankfully he had refrained from asking any more awkward questions, although she sensed that his curiosity simmered under the outward charm.

'If you have any thoughts about Charlie, I'd be pleased to hear them,' Conor said, interrupting her reverie as they headed back to the surgery on a grey, wet Friday afternoon.

Their last visit had been to a man in his early sixties, physically healthy but suffering from depression. Conor had explained how Charlie had spent his life farming, building up a reputation for a prize herd of Ayrshire cattle, only to lose everything when the area had been hit by an outbreak of foot and mouth disease. With his stock culled, his life's work decimated, his farm silent and lifeless, Charlie had given up. Increasingly lethargic, he refused to take an interest in anything, rarely speaking and not eating properly. He had no family but his loyal friends were worried. So, Kate knew, was Conor.

'It's horribly sad.' She imagined how different Charlie must have been when full of vigour and enthusiasm compared with the shell of the man she had just met. 'Losing everything that way, his whole purpose for being.'

'I know. I don't want to impose something drastic on him at this stage and risk alienating him. At the moment he'll let me in, take his medication, but he won't consider seeing our visiting counsellor, Sarah Baxter. The situation has worsened since Christmas.'

'What happened at Christmas?'

'His dog died.' Conor sighed. 'Max had been keeping Charlie going. After losing him, he just sat down and became even more uncommunicative.'

Having come to know more about Conor as a doctor in the last few days, she could tell how frustrated he was, feeling he had been unable to help Charlie through this difficult time. 'I'll give it some thought,' she promised as they arrived back at the surgery, pondering on the problem as she preceded him inside. They heard a fearful screaming echoing down the corridor from the direction of the nurses' treatment room.

'I'm so glad you're back,' a harassed Aileen greeted them. 'Conor, can you do anything?'

'What's the problem?' he asked, handing over the patient notes for filing.

'Little Callie McIntosh.' The practice manager grimaced. 'She's cut her arm and it needs stitching but she won't let anyone near her. Fred has tried, so have Dorothy and the other nurses, Kristen and Sandra.'

Kate went with Conor to the treatment room but hesitated in the doorway, the young girl's distress stirring unwanted memories and making her feel panicky. About three, the child was red-faced from screaming, a mix of fear and fury in her wide blue eyes, a bloodstained dressing roughly wrapped round one arm. Callie's mother was frazzled, while nurse practitioner Dorothy's look of relief when she saw Conor was comical. Feeling more in control as she forced herself to concentrate on the present, thankful Conor had not noticed her momentary lapse, Kate watched as he took charge. Talking to calm Callie, he knelt down beside her, smiled and turned his attention to the child's well-loved teddy bear, which was clutched tightly in the hand of her un-injured arm.

'What's his name?'

'B-Bear,' she whispered.

'It looks like Bear needs a little help.' Conor pointed to a split in the seam of one leg where the filling was poking through. 'Shall I make him better?'

Wide-eyed, Callie nodded. 'Can you?'

'Sure I can. A few quick stitches and he'll be as good as new.'

Amazed, Kate looked on as Conor pretended to give the teddy a local anaesthetic and then swiftly put a few stitches in the furry leg. She knew how pushed he was for time, and yet he gave of himself to this troubled child. It was a side of him she had never anticipated but was now coming to know so well.

'There!' He smiled when he was done. 'That wasn't dif-

ficult, was it? And Bear was so brave. Do you think you can
be as clever as him and let me make you better, too?'

'S'pose.'

'Good girl.'

There were a few more tears but Conor talked to Callie,
working gently but swiftly, and the job was soon finished. The
little girl even had a smile on her tear-stained face as Conor
proudly stuck a colourful sticker on her T-shirt for being so
brave and gave her a sugar-free lollipop.

'What a star,' he praised, ruffling the blonde curls.

Unsettled, Kate left Conor talking over Callie's follow-up
care with her mother and Dorothy, slipping away to the staffroom to help herself to a quick mug of hot chocolate before
her first afternoon appointment arrived. For once the room
was empty and, while the kettle boiled, she browsed the huge
pinboard stuffed with photos of the staff from holidays and
various activities which she had not had the chance to look
at before. Her attention caught, she paused to examine one
photo more closely, her eyes widening in surprise. Unless she
was mistaken it was of Conor, completely bald, posing with
a young girl wearing a headscarf.

'We tease Conor about that,' Aileen informed, startling her.
'But we were very proud of him. He has a special way with
people.'

'What happened?' Kate asked, interested despite her determination not to get involved.

'About four years ago Conor was caring for Lucy, a
thirteen-year-old with cancer. She was terrified about the
treatment, tearful about her looks and losing her hair, so
Conor did a deal with her—said he'd shave his head in
support to keep her company.'

Unwanted emotion welled inside her at yet more evidence
of Conor's caring. She didn't know many doctors who would
go to those lengths for someone.

'We always say Conor should be available on the NHS

by prescription!' Aileen joked. 'He's wonderful at making people feel better about themselves. You wouldn't believe the number of patients who have benefited from Conor giving them some time, be it a game of golf, a trip out somewhere or just a chat at home.'

Kate wondered if some of the teasing about 'dates' referred to this and not to romantic entanglements at all. She had discovered firsthand how special time with Conor could make a person feel, having been on the receiving end of some of that one-to-one attention herself that week. She didn't want to admit that the intimate smiles and warm looks made her insides throb with desire and made her wish for things that were out of bounds.

'I'm surprised he doesn't have a family of his own, given how good he is with children,' Kate ventured, annoyed with herself for fishing.

'There'd be many a lady applying for that job!' Aileen laughed. 'Conor's not serious about any of his dates so I can't see that happening.'

After Aileen had gone, Kate made her drink, cradling her mug in her hands, a frown on her face. What had she expected? She had heard enough about Conor to confirm her opinion of him as a womaniser who was shy of commitment. Not that it mattered to her. The way he ran his life was none of her business, but it was warning enough, if any more was needed, to redouble her guard against his easy charm.

Her frown deepening, she returned to the photos, her gaze straying to another one of Conor, this time with two other gorgeous-looking men, walking out on the hills. Her gaze moved on, lingering on a photo of someone in a protective body suit and helmet, holding some kind of tray-like object, taken at a winter sports centre.

'What on earth is that?' she murmured to herself, leaning in for a closer inspection.

'Hi.'

She jumped, nearly dropping her mug as Conor's husky voice sounded in her ear, so close his breath fanned her cheek. She stepped away, horribly aware of him, his earthy fragrance teasing her senses, her pulse racing. 'I didn't hear you come in.'

'Sorry.' His teasing smile belied his apology. 'Fancy having a go with me?'

'I beg your pardon?'

His smile widened at her wary suspicion and he pointed to the photo she had been looking at, then the one next to it of the figure sledging down an ice chute.

'That's you?'

'It is.'

'You flung yourself head first down an ice track on a teatray?' Kate gasped in amazement.

'It's not a teatray!' Laughing, he stepped up close behind her, looking over her shoulder. Her body tingled in response. 'It's an expensive, high-tech piece of equipment called a skeleton bob, and it's fun.'

'It's barking mad crazy is what it is. And "skeleton" is an accurate description of what you'd be if you did it. Why don't you play football or golf like a normal person?'

He laughed again and she could feel the rumble of it against her back. 'I do those, too… I love sport. I go curling, mountain-biking, walking, all sorts.'

No wonder he was so fit, his body so superbly athletic. Anxious at the way she was reacting to the proximity of that body, scared she would weaken and forget the many reasons why she had to resist him, she slid to the side and put more space between them, her heart hammering as she concentrated on washing up her mug, keeping her gaze averted.

'Kate,' he murmured, his voice huskily intimate. 'I wanted to ask you—'

'There you both are!' Jenny announced, appearing in the doorway, and Kate breathed sigh of relief at the reprieve.

Conor sounded anything but relieved, frustration ringing in his tone. 'What's the problem, Jenny?'

'There's no problem.' The young receptionist smiled, oblivious of the charged atmosphere. 'Kate, Fred wants to see you in his room before you begin your consultations.'

'Thanks, Jenny. I'm finished here.'

She dried her hands, refusing to look at Conor, and headed for the door, hearing Jenny's eager invitation behind her.

'Conor, some of us are getting together for a drink after work. Will you come?'

'I'm sorry but I already have plans tonight. Another time, though, I promise.'

'It's OK if you have a date. Which lucky lady has drawn the winning ticket this time?' Jenny teased, although disappointment underlaid the joking.

Conor murmured something Kate couldn't catch then added, 'I can't let her down, Jenny.'

She walked on, thankful to hear no more of the conversation. Professionally he was an incredible doctor but privately he was a player, a natural flirt, and the last thing she needed was another one of those in her life. Squaring her shoulders, determined to push thoughts of Conor from her mind, she knocked on Fred's door and stepped inside.

'Kate's here now, James. Yes, we're delighted,' Fred said enthusiastically over the phone. 'I'll pass you over and give you some time to talk.' Putting his hand over the mouthpiece, he stood up and smiled. 'James would like a word with you, my dear. Take your time. I'll go and get myself a cup of tea before surgery and give you some privacy.'

'Thank you, Fred.'

She waited until the door closed then picked up the phone, moving to stare out of the window at the view down a side road towards the sea.

'Kate?' a familiar voice barked in her ear.

'I'm here, James. How are you?'

'Busy. I phoned to hear how your first week has been,' he said without preamble. 'How have you been coping?'

'Things haven't been as bad as I anticipated...so far.'

'Kate, nothing is going to change what happened but you *can* change how you react to it. You're a wonderful doctor and Glentown-on-Firth is the perfect place for you to ease back into work and find some peace with yourself.'

'I guess time will tell,' she allowed, wishing she could feel as confident about herself and her abilities as the prof and her father did.

'The circumstances were extraordinary, Kate, you can't blame yourself,' the prof chastised for the umpteenth time. 'Anyone would have been traumatised by what happened. Most would never have lasted as long as you did, kept their heads and saved so many lives.'

Kate bit her lip. It was easy for other people to tell her what she should and shouldn't have done, how she should and shouldn't feel, but they hadn't been there. No one else knew what it had been like. She had been back in the UK for two months and she still had nightmares, still doubted her decisions...still grieved. Grieved for Wesley, her brother, for the colleagues and patients she felt she had failed. She may have healed physically but she hadn't come close to dealing with the memories and self-doubt.

'I don't have all day, Kate.' His impatient voice snapped her from her thoughts. 'I'm due in Theatre in an hour. An interesting case, multiple fractures. A shame you aren't here, I could use you.'

A cold shiver ran along her spine. 'You know I can't do that. I'll never do surgery again.'

'I think you're wrong but I accept that's your choice. Now, how are you finding everyone up there?'

'Fred's lovely.' She smiled, already fond of the paternal doctor. 'The other staff have been very welcoming.'

'Including Conor Anderson?' he queried, amusement in his gravelly voice.

'You knew about him, didn't you?' A hint of accusation laced her tone. 'Conor is like Darren all over again.'

'Don't talk such bloody rubbish.' The prof seldom minced his words and Kate couldn't prevent a smile as she imagined his fierce blue eyes, the bushy grey brows knotted together in annoyance. She remembered how terrified she had been when she had first met Professor James Fielding-Smythe during her training, a man whose reputation, not only as a peerless surgeon but as a taskmaster able to reduce the toughest of junior doctors to a trembling wreck with one withering glance or cutting word, was legendary. Since then he had become a trusted adviser. 'Conor Anderson is as far from Darren as it is possible to be. He's a special doctor, Kate. He could be good for you.'

'I gather Conor's a little too good to all the women around here,' she riposted with asperity.

'I doubt the man's a monk but that doesn't make him the kind of unscrupulous, cheating bastard Darren proved to be. Sacking him was the best decision I made—and the most satisfying,' he added with a ruthless chuckle. Kate winced as she recalled the terrible scene. 'My worst decision was letting you leave my team to return to general practice and then back your yen to join the aid agency. I should have fought to keep you. You had the makings of a first-class surgeon.'

Kate swallowed. Sometimes she wished the professor wasn't quite so blunt. 'James—'

'I've known Fred Murdoch nearly forty years, we trained together, fulfilled the best-man role for each other when we married our respective wives,' he informed her, his voice turning reminiscent as he moved the conversation in a fresh direction, giving her little time to adjust her thoughts. 'I may have told you that Cordelia and I visit Glentown-on-Firth every year. Fred and I have a week or two salmon fishing. Our

wives enjoyed shopping trips to Edinburgh or Glasgow—
until Fred's wife, Annette, died two years ago. Cancer. Very
quick. Conor was a tremendous support to Fred when Annette
was ill. And afterwards. Give him a chance. More impor-
tantly, give yourself a chance.'

'I'm trying to. I'm not sure I still have what it takes to
be a doctor.'

'You must find that out for yourself. Being a GP was
always your original goal but you were sidetracked by Darren
and his ambitions. Make the most of this fresh start, Kate.'

The professor hung up with customary abruptness after in-
structing her to send regular email reports on her progress.
Kate stared at the phone feeling unsettled and confused,
James's wise if impatient advice ringing in her ears. A tap on
the door announced Fred's return and she looked up as he
came back into the room. She had not known about his wife
and a wave of compassion washed over her as she studied
him, seeing an underlying tiredness, noticing the way his suit
hung on him as if he had shrunk from the person he had once
been.

'All right, my dear? Jenny told me the call was finished.'

'I'm fine,' she fibbed. 'Thank you.'

Fred moved to his desk and sat down, his expression be-
nevolent but curious. 'Kate, I'm not going to pry but James
mentioned that you wanted to come here because you needed
to think about some changes in your life and to decide on the
direction of your career.'

'Something like that, yes,' she managed, uncomfortable
under the gentle regard.

'I hope you will come to think of us as your friends. If
there is ever a time you would like to talk, about anything at
all, I hope you will feel you can come to me. Or Conor—most
of you young women seem to gravitate to him!'

Kate closed her eyes, ignoring his final words. 'Thank you,
Fred.'

Emotion threatened to choke her at the feeling she was there under false presences and was taking advantage of this man's kindness.

CHAPTER FOUR

LOCKING up the surgery on Sunday morning, Conor slipped the keys in his pocket and walked round to the flat. Out on calls on Friday and in the staffroom later, he had felt closer to Kate than at any time during the week and he was frustrated that Jenny had interrupted them. He had not seen Kate since but when he had phoned her a while ago to tell her he was downstairs, she had been tense, her voice distant.

He hesitated at the front door, pondering the wisdom of his actions. Kate had not given him the slightest encouragement but he couldn't keep away from her. Before he could change his mind, he rang the bell, his pulse rate increasing when he heard footsteps on the stairs, his breath burning in his lungs when she opened the door looking soft, cuddly and vulnerable. It was the first time he had seen her out of the smart suits she wore to work, and the figure-hugging jeans teamed with a white shirt that offset the olive tones of her skin had the ever-present desire tightening inside him.

'Hi.' He smiled, resisting the urge to touch her. 'May I come in?'

Wary indecision shadowed her dark brown eyes. After several moments she stepped back, turning and heading up the stairs, leaving him to close the door and follow in her wake, puzzled by her renewed defensiveness. He had a great relationship with his colleagues, friends and patients. And he loved women. All women. He enjoyed their company but he was very choosy about who he became involved with. It sounded corny but he was looking for the one woman he could spend the rest of his life with and with whom he could have the family he craved. His social life was active but he rarely took things further than friendship.

The scars of the past had deep roots and after the disaster of his parents' marriage and their subsequent succession of partners and failed relationships he was determined not to settle for second best, not to repeat their mistakes. He'd thought he'd found his ideal woman once, at med school, but fed up with the long hours and his desire to be a rural GP his girlfriend had dumped him for someone richer and more upwardly mobile. He'd learned the lesson. And the padlock round his heart had never been opened again. He had planned it would stay locked until *the one* came along. If she didn't, he would bitterly regret not having children but better that than raise them in the kind of broken and unhappy home he had endured.

It was amazing, inconvenient and unsettling, but he had known from the first second he'd met her that Kate was *the one*. Disapproval and distrust registered in her soulful brown eyes whenever she looked at him—which wasn't often as her gaze was usually fixed on some point behind his shoulder or down at the floor. It would be easy to retreat from that touch-me-not front, but he was intrigued by her and sensed that, like an iceberg, much more of her lay below the surface than she ever allowed the world to see. Concerned for her well-being, he was determined to find the real Kate. He knew she was worth fighting for. Whether he could ever win her round was another matter entirely. Filled with nervous uncertainty, he watched her now, arms folded across her chest, every atom of her being tense, the shadow of pain dulling her lonely brown eyes. Everything about her drew him like a moth to a flame.

'What do you want?'

He swallowed down an inappropriate chuckle. Better not tell her how badly he wanted to take her to bed. 'I'm sorry I disturbed you earlier, but I didn't want you to worry if you heard noises downstairs.'

'That was thoughtful, thank you,' she allowed, unbending a little. 'Was everything all right?'

'Allan Mountford, a farmer from outside the village, cut himself on some machinery and his leg needed stitching. It's such a long drive to A and E so it makes sense to take care of it here. Easier and quicker for everyone.'

'Except for you.' A slight frown creased the smoothness of her brow. 'I thought the service handled out-of-hours work.'

'Officially it does,' he admitted, looking away from her, embarrassed to admit how he couldn't let go. 'Fred needed to cut back his hours so I went along with his choice to sign on with the service, but I like to keep up with my own patients. I tend to take some evening and weekend calls.'

'I see.'

He could tell from her tone that the information didn't square with her image of him. He walked across to the window and admired the view. 'Are you all right here alone?' he murmured, hating to think of her by herself. Lonely.

'Some people like being alone,' she pointed out coolly. 'Not everyone has to have company all the time or needs to be the centre of attention.'

'Ouch!' He turned to face her, his smile rueful. 'You don't approve of me, do you?'

'I don't know you.'

He captured her unwilling gaze. 'So why not reserve judgement until you do?'

'Conor—'

'You're an excellent doctor, Kate. Why do you doubt yourself?'

She looked scared, her eyes widening with alarm. 'I don't know what you mean,' she riposted in that stiff, cool tone he was coming to know so well, the one she used when she wanted to keep people at bay or avoid something…or when she was lying. At the moment she was doing all three.

'I think you do.'

'I— I was thinking about Charlie.' Panic brought an edge to her voice and a desperation to her eyes, her fingers nervously tucking a few silken strands of hair behind her ear as she changed the subject. 'Your farmer.'

Aching for whatever was eating her up inside, he moved closer, taking her trembling hand in his, feeling the rapid and uneven beat of the pulse at her wrist. 'I know who Charlie is, Kate.'

'You mentioned his dog.' Her voice was husky as she slipped her fingers from his and stepped away.

'Yes.' Disappointed, he allowed her retreat. 'Max had been Charlie's constant companion for fourteen years. Losing him at Christmas was the final straw.'

'Perhaps it's time he had a new dog, a new life to worry about. So he feels needed.'

He thrust his hands into his pockets to stop himself reaching for her again. 'It's not something he'll talk about.'

'But if he was faced with it, if someone presented him with a dog that has had a bad start or been rescued from something and needs someone special to give it a home and care and…'

Her words trailed off, her troubled gaze flicking to his then away again, and he had the sudden knowledge there was a resonance here, maybe one she had not intended but which had hit her too—a damaged life that needed healing. Just like Kate. Kate, who so clearly needed some loving care but was unable to reach out and take what he so desperately wanted to give her. Sensing her unease, he forced himself to focus on Charlie, realising that it was not only an excellent plan but was a way he could involve Kate and spend time with her outside work.

'You're brilliant!' He smiled at the surprise on her face. 'It's definitely worth a try. And I know just the person who can help us.'

Aware of her watching him, wary but interested, he took out his mobile phone and brought up a number from the memory, waiting several moments until the call was answered.

'Is that the Lochanrig home for waifs and strays?'

'Conor?' The voice registered a mix of harassment, welcome and laughter.

'Hello, Hannah. I need your help. You know that puppy you were telling me about? Have you found a home for him yet?'

'Nic thought he'd found somewhere a couple of weeks ago but it fell through,' Hannah informed him. 'I wish we could keep him but he's causing havoc with Wallace!'

Knowing what a character their ginger cat was, Conor laughed. 'I think I might have the perfect home for the puppy if you are interested.'

'That would be fantastic. Have you really?'

'It's all thanks to Kate, our new doctor,' he continued, winking at her as he explained Charlie's situation. 'Is the puppy ready to home?'

'The sooner the better!' Hannah laughed, sounding frazzled again.

'Would it be OK if we came over and collected him today?'

'Sure. Come to lunch, Conor. We'd love to see you. And meet your Kate!'

'Unfortunately not. Yet.'

'Oh, dear!' Hannah sounded knowing and amused. 'Like that, is it?'

His looked at Kate and the customary wave of longing swamped him. One week and his entire life had been turned upside down. 'Yeah, it is. See you in a while, Hannah.'

* * *

Kate shifted under the heat of desire in Conor's green eyes as he looked at her before ending his call. It was hard enough coping with her own confused feelings for him, the physical want warring with emotional doubt, knowing he was the last man on earth she should let close to her because she would find herself back in the painful place she had been before. Conor had the power to hurt her. And at the moment she was too vulnerable, her life too shaky, to take the temporary pleasure he would offer.

She was taken by surprise as he hugged her and dropped a brief kiss on her cheek before letting her go, his touch leaving her skin tingling.

'You're a star, Kate. Come on, grab your things, we can go now.'

'What? But—'

'You have to come,' he protested before she could summon an excuse. 'It was your idea and I'll need some help with the puppy on the drive back.'

Bemused, Kate found herself railroaded into accompanying him, with time only to pull on a knee-length cardigan, ankle boots and collect her bag. She had to be mad, spending more time with Conor, she fretted, confused by him, thrown by his insight and probing questions, alarmed by her unwanted physical reaction to him. As they drove east out of Glentown-on-Firth towards the larger town of Rigtownbrae some miles away, she felt tongue-tied, unable to think of any subject outside their work environment that was safe. Impatient and annoyed with herself, she looked out of the window at the impressive landscape.

'I didn't get a chance to catch up with you on Friday.' Conor's voice drew her from her thoughts. 'I was going to ask you to come with me in the evening.'

Shocked, she stared at him. He'd planned on taking her out on his date? She opened her mouth to speak but could think of nothing appropriate and closed it again. The man had some nerve! How could he be so brazen about it?

'What's wrong?'

'Nothing,' she murmured, unable to keep the terseness from her voice. 'Why would I have wanted to go with you?'

A laugh rumbled from inside him. 'You certainly know how to deflate an ego!'

'Conor…' She sucked in a deep breath and closed her eyes. The man was impossible.

'Anyway,' he continued, undaunted by her manner, 'I went over to the county infirmary to visit Lizzie.'

Kate opened her eyes and stared at him in amazement. 'You went to see Lizzie?'

'Of course. That's what I was trying to tell you in the staffroom.'

'On Friday?'

He glanced at her with a puzzled frown. 'That's right. I thought you might be interested.'

'I am.' She struggled to find her voice, confused by the feelings churning inside her: shame that she had misjudged him again; pleasure that he had not only taken time to see the elderly lady but that he had considered taking her with him; stupid relief that he had not been out smooching with one of his women. 'How is she?'

'Holding her own and in good spirits.'

'I'm so pleased. She's a lovely lady,' Kate enthused, not wanting to examine why her own spirits had suddenly lifted.

'She is.' Pulling up to negotiate a road junction, he glanced at her and smiled. 'It's too soon to know what the long-term prognosis will be but I was pleased to find her coping so well. I'll let you know next time I'm going over and if you want to come, you'd be welcome.'

A warm feeling settled inside her. 'Thanks. So what is this place we're going to today?' she ventured after a few moments, trying to steer things on to safer ground.

'Lochanrig is a village about eight miles north-east of Rigtownbrae. Hannah Frost has been GP there for some years—her grandfather founded the practice and her father carried it on. Nic di Angelis is Italian and he arrived about eighteen months ago as a locum and swept reserved, workaholic Hannah off her feet! They've been married about nine months now, although Hannah keeps Frost as her working name to avoid confusion.'

'I see.' Kate tried to absorb all the information. 'So what do they have to do with this puppy?'

Conor chuckled again. 'They are always taking in waifs and strays. Nic rescued the first one not long after he arrived, the only survivor of a litter of kittens he found dumped in a sack by the road.'

'How awful.'

'Wallace is a real character! They've acquired various other animals in the intervening months and they told me about this puppy recently. He'll be about four or five months old now,' he explained, negotiating the main street of Rigtownbrae, nearly deserted on a sleepy Sunday, before taking the rural lanes towards Lochanrig. 'I thought of it when you had your brainwave about Charlie. This may well be just what he needs.'

When they arrived at a large stone-built house set in its own grounds on the edge of Lochanrig village, the front door was open, an adapted child gate covered in wire mesh blocking the gap. Conor rang the bell and a disembodied voice greeted them from inside, vying with the distant barking of a dog.

'Conor, if that's you, I'm in the kitchen. Please, shut the gate after you!'

Stepping back to let her through ahead of him, Conor guided her inside, closing the inner door and the gate behind them. Kate was conscious of his hand at the small of her back, steering her towards a door that led to a large, airy country kitchen where an attractive woman with long chestnut hair, tied back in a loose ponytail, was sitting at a rustic table, a cloth draped over one shoulder, a tiny scrap of tabby fur cradled in her hands.

'Hi. Nearly finished.' She smiled as the kitten took the last of its milk.

Kate watched, fascinated, as the woman gently wiped the kitten's face then rose to her feet and set it back inside a large pen that already contained a bundle of assorted-coloured kittens, and she tried to count how many there were in the tangle of legs. Five. As Hannah moved to wash her hands, Kate edged across to take a closer look at the tiny bodies. They were so gorgeous. She turned round to ask Hannah about them, in time to see the woman laugh as Conor swept her into his arms for a hug. The insidious curl of jealousy that clenched inside her was dismaying. She didn't want to feel anything. It was ridiculous. Conor was of no interest to her beyond work and Hannah was happily married to someone else.

'It's good to see you, Conor,' Hannah said. 'Sorry about the muddle.'

Keeping his arm around the woman's waist and cuddling her close, Conor peered into the pen. 'Are you going to keep any of them?'

'Would you believe me if I said no?'

'Nope!'

Hannah pushed a fall of escaped chestnut waves back from her face. 'I thought not. I get so attached but I know we can't keep them all. It's not possible. It's only been eighteen months and we've already got Wallace, Hoppity, Sparky, the puppy and now these kittens. Someone rescued them from being drowned and brought them to us because we've earned a reputation for not turning anything away. I dread to think what Nic's going to bring home next! Speaking of whom, he had to pop out to see a patient—he'll be back soon.'

'I'm already here,' an accented voice announced from behind them, and Kate looked round to see a stunningly good-looking man approach, recognising him from one of the photos with Conor on the pinboard in the staffroom back at Glentown.

Conor sighed in mock disappointment. 'I suppose you want your wife back?'

'When you can spare her,' the dark-haired man agreed wryly.

As Conor released Hannah, Kate was surprised when the men shared a brief, manly hug before the sexy Italian took Hannah in his arms and kissed her.

'Kate, come and meet Nic and Hannah,' Conor invited, drawing her closer, reigniting her awareness as he rested a hand at her waist. 'This is Kate Fisher, our new doctor.'

'Welcome to the madhouse, Kate.' Hannah laughed.

The couple were friendly and fun, but Kate couldn't halt the lingering envy at how clearly they loved each other, how tactile they were, always touching, sharing private glances.

'How were the Pattersons?' Hannah asked, moving to the oven to check on the delicious-smelling chicken that was roasting.

'Sandy is deteriorating,' Nic admitted sadly. 'Alexandra is coping as only she can.'

Hannah drew her hair back from her face and retied the rough ponytail. 'Alex is amazing. She gave up her job as a district nurse in the south of England to come home and care for her dad and keep their small farm going,' she explained to them as Nic left the room. 'I've no idea how she manages everything. We don't know how long Sandy has, but Alex will be there to the last. I don't suppose you have any nurse vacancies coming up, do you?'

Conor shook his head. 'Not right now. Why?'

'As and when the time comes, Alex is going to need a job. We'd take her ourselves, she's terrific, but we're not likely to have any places either. If it comes to it I'll have a word with Kyle and see if there's anything going in Rigtownbrae. Not that

I'd wish anyone on poison Penny. She's a district nurse there,' Hannah explained at Kate's murmur of curiosity, the accompanying grimace implying that easygoing Hannah had a problem with the nurse. Before she could question her, Hannah turned to Conor and moved on. 'Have you seen Kyle lately?'

'Last Monday,' Conor confirmed, getting his wrist slapped as he tried to help himself to a roast potato. Kate hid a smile as he winked at her. 'We went walking.'

'How is he?'

'Low. The whole marriage and pregnancy thing has hit him hard on top of everything else.' A disapproving frown darkened his face and Kate wondered what the story was with his friend, deflated by further evidence of Conor's antipathy to lasting relationships and families.

Nic returned, having changed into jeans and jumper. 'Is Kyle coming to the charity dinner?'

'I doubt it,' Conor replied. 'I don't think he's ready for anything like that. You're both going, right?'

Hannah nodded and smiled at her. 'Are you coming, Kate?'

'I don't know anything about it,' she admitted, feeling uncomfortable.

'Of course she is,' Conor protested.

Kate glared at him. 'I don't think so.'

'She will.'

'Conor—'

'Why not come and see the rest of the menagerie while we wait for lunch to be ready?' Hannah suggested, and Kate was grateful for the change of subject.

'We've had to separate them. The puppy is in the dining room—he and Wallace don't get on. Sparky, Hoppity and Wally are in the living room.'

Hannah opened the door to be greeted by an enthusiastic Border terrier and Kate looked around the spacious room, seeing an elegant ginger cat curled up on a cushion on the settee enjoying the sunshine that streamed through the window.

'This is Wallace,' Nic said, stroking the ginger cat who began purring like a road drill. Smiling, Nic moved across and picked up a small black and white cat which, to her surprise, was wearing a colourful jumper. Amused at her reaction, Nic cradled the little cat in his arms as he continued. 'Meet Sparky. He was badly burned but is healing well. He is the proud owner of many woolly jumpers knitted for him by the local Women's Rural! He must wear them until his skin settles and his hair begins to grow back.'

As Hannah dropped to the floor to cuddle the energetic little dog, Kate turned to watch, listening as the story of how the sandy-haired terrier had come to them was recounted.

'Hoppity had a horrible time with her injuries,' Hannah began, gently stroking the dog's rough coat as it climbed into her lap. 'Nic found her quite by chance. She'd been caught fast in some fencing wire and several times we were scared she might die. She had to have her leg amputated, but it's never slowed her down or stopped her doing anything.' Hannah smiled but Kate felt familiar panic overwhelming her. 'You'd never know, would you? She's amazing.'

Listening to the story of the brave little dog's struggle for survival, Conor glanced at Kate, frowning as he found her staring into space, her face pale. Exchanging a puzzled glance with Hannah and Nic, he moved across to her.

'You OK?' he murmured, grateful that his friends continued to fuss over the animals and chat as if nothing unusual was happening.

Kate, however, didn't respond. She appeared to be in some kind of trance and he took her hand, finding it shaking and cold. Concerned, he gently squeezed her fingers. 'Kate?'

She blinked, slowly focusing on him, the trauma and hurt

in her eyes making him want to take her in his arms and make everything better.

'What's wrong, sweetheart?'

'Nothing.'

That cool, stiff voice again. 'Kate—'

'I'm fine.' She snatched her hand free and crouched down beside Hannah to make a fuss of Hoppity.

He didn't believe her for a second but under the circumstances, with Nic and Hannah looking on, there was little he could do about it at the moment. What had happened? Worried, he thought back over the conversation but nothing struck him as unusual or likely to have upset Kate to that extent. It was clearly nothing to do with being scared of the dog because she was now taking the wriggling body from Hannah and cuddling it against her. The first genuine smile he had seen from her curved her mouth as Hoppity nuzzled inside the long pale blue cardigan she had pulled on over her shirt and jeans and began licking her face, the stubby tail wagging furiously. He shoved his hands in his pockets, cursing himself as all kinds of fool for being jealous of a dog, for goodness' sake! And the smile did crazy things to his insides. He'd waited all week for it and only wished she would look at him like that.

When Hannah and Kate rose to their feet and moved out of the room to go and inspect the puppy they had come to collect for Charlie, Nic gave Sparky a final cuddle and set him back on the floor to play with a toy.

'What was that about with Kate?' he asked with concern.

'I have no idea.'

'She reminds me a little of Hannah when I first met her.'

Interested, Conor glanced at Nic. 'In what way?'

'She is sad inside.'

'I know.'

Nic moved to the settee and made a fuss of Wallace. 'I do not forget you, little man. Come, Conor, we go and see your puppy, yes?' he suggested, leading the way out of the room and closing the door. 'So what is Kate's story?'

'That I don't know—yet.' They paused in the dining-room doorway and his gaze settled on Kate where she fussed over a young tri-colour Border collie. 'But I intend to find out.'

Nic's smile was amused. 'That is the way of it?'

'It is,' Conor admitted ruefully. 'Not that I'm getting very far. But I knew the second I first saw her. I shook her hand and it was like being plugged into the national grid.'

'For me also.' Nic's dark eyes filled with love as he looked at his wife. 'It just took us a while to get there.'

'Kate's worth waiting for. I'm just not sure what to do, how things will work out.'

'Mmm!'

He glanced at Nic and caught his grin. 'What's funny?'

'The mysterious way these things work. Usually you are fighting women off with a stick.'

'It's not like that,' Conor protested with an embarrassed laugh. 'You make me sound like some kind of gigolo!'

Nic's expression sobered. 'Not at all, my friend. They may chase you but I know you never encourage them and seldom follow up on the attention. But now, how do you say, the boot is on the other foot? For the first time you have to do the chasing, no?' he teased in his lilting, accented voice.

'Nic, could you bear to go and check on the chicken while I tell them about puppy?' Hannah called, turning to smile at them and bringing their quiet talk to an end.

'Of course, *cara*.' Nic turned and rested a hand on Conor's shoulder. 'If it is meant to be, so it will be.'

Nic left on his errand and Conor moved further into the room, eager not to be too far from Kate, doubt and uncertainty remaining despite his friend's advice.

'We'd keep him ourselves,' Hannah was explaining and he tried to set his thoughts aside and concentrate on the puppy. 'But aside from the fact that Wally hates him for some reason, working the hours we do and with the new orphan kittens we just don't have the time needed to devote to another dog. And he'll need much more attention than little Hoppity.'

'What happened to him?' Conor asked, as Kate knelt beside the shy young dog. He noticed how calm and gentle she was, taking care not to touch the healing wounds on the thin, gangly body.

Hannah grimaced and looked up at him. 'Believe me, you really don't want to know.'

'That bad?'

'Worse. I've never seen Nic so angry.' Hannah shook her head. 'The puppy was a horrible mess when we first brought him home, Conor, but he has plenty of spirit and a strong will to live. He's been under the care of Alistair Brown, the vet in Rigtownbrae. Alistair is happy for the puppy to go home now as it's just a matter of healing. And time. And plenty of tender loving care.'

'I think he's going to give Charlie a whole new purpose in life,' Conor commented, wishing his job allowed him to keep the dog himself. 'Is he still on medication?'

'Yes, but he's good to go. I've written everything out. Is Charlie going to be able to take him back to Alistair for a check-up in a couple of weeks before transferring to your local vet?'

'I'll take them both myself if necessary,' Conor promised.

'And if it doesn't work with Charlie?' Hannah worried. 'What will happen to the puppy then?'

'I'll let you know every step of the way what happens. I have a plan B, but if it turns out Charlie doesn't come round then I can always bring the puppy back to you if that's what you choose.'

Hannah nodded, her eyes misting. 'I purposely didn't name him because I knew he couldn't stay, but I'm going to miss the little chap.'

'Come and visit. You and Nic haven't been over in a while. We'd love to see you.'

'That would be good.' Hannah brightened. 'We'll organise something. Are you going to cook?'

Conor smiled. 'If you're nice to me.'

'Your fish pie?'

'If that's what you want!'

'Has Conor cooked for you yet?' Hannah asked Kate, and he watched as Kate shook her head, concentrating on the dog.

'I'm just here to work.'

'You have to eat!' Hannah exclaimed, brushing the protest aside and glancing up at him with a querying frown. 'And you haven't lived if you haven't tasted Conor's food.'

Kate looked up then and he smiled at her surprise. Clearly, being able to cook was something else that didn't fit with the distorted image she had of him, along with cuddling babies and rehoming animals. 'I'll be pleased to display my culinary skills any time, Kate.'

Kate kept her eyes averted, not wanting to think about Conor's skills, culinary or otherwise. It was far too dangerous. She was relieved when Nic called them from the kitchen and Conor sauntered off ahead to join him.

'Conor's great, isn't he?' Hannah smiled, casting her a inquisitive glance.

'I don't really know him.' Flustered, Kate focused on the puppy. 'He's a good doctor.'

'That's for sure. The best.'

Her own curiosity getting the better of her, Kate risked some probing of her own. 'Did the two of you date or something?'

'Goodness, no! Whatever gave you that idea?'

'You just seem…close,' she murmured, embarrassed and wishing she hadn't asked.

Hannah sat back on her heels, her expression sobering. 'I didn't date anyone. I wouldn't even have been able to hug Conor a year or two ago,' she told her, and Kate listened in growing horror as the other woman gave her a brief account of what had happened to her at medical school.

'That's appalling, Hannah.'

'It seems another life away now. Thanks to Nic.' A loving, satisfied smile curved her mouth and her green eyes twinkled. 'I was so scared and I put up a fight but he won me round in the end. Thank goodness!' Hannah paused a moment as she settled the puppy back in his large open pen full of toys then turned to smile at her. 'Conor's very like Nic that way.'

'How do you mean?'

'The need to care for anyone or anything they see hurting.' Hannah's words were direct as they both rose to their feet. 'Take it from one who knows, Kate. Don't run too hard: it is so worth being caught. I never imagined I could be this happy, this whole.'

Kate looked away from the other woman's understanding smile, feeling uncomfortable as they walked back to the kitchen. She couldn't imagine ever feeling whole again. As she took her place next to Conor at the table in the kitchen she sensed him looking at her, nervous when his hand reached for hers, warm and gentle as he gave her fingers a brief squeeze.

'OK?'

'Fine,' she fibbed.

She heard his sigh but was thankful that he released her hand, although she remained tinglingly conscious of his presence close beside her.

Lunch was delicious. She listened more than she talked as the conversation and laughter flowed around her, unable to get Hannah's words and experiences out of her mind. As they lingered over coffee after the meal, she met Nic's kind but knowing gaze, seeing the speculation in his dark eyes, relieved when Conor drew the Italian's attention, chatting to him about motorbikes as he flipped through the latest copy of *Performance Bikes* magazine that sat on top of a pile of medical journals at one end of the table.

'You haven't got the new Ducatti?' Conor exclaimed, awe and envy in his tone.

'I have. You want to come and see it?' Conor was already on his feet and Nic laughed as he turned to Hannah. 'You do not mind, do you, *cara?*'

Hannah rolled her eyes in mock despair. 'Bloody motor-bikes. And typical men. Leave us poor women to do the washing-up!'

'My wife jokes with you.' Nic smiled with amused indulgence. 'She has turned into something of a biker chick herself.'

'I have not!' Hannah protested at his teasing.

'No? You do not beg to share a ride with me, *innamorata?*'

Kate saw Hannah's cheeks warm in response to her husband's suggestive murmur, the look passing between them leaving her in little doubt at the hidden meanings and sexy undertones.

'Go and look at the damn bike.' Hannah laughed, pushing him towards the door.

Kate discovered that Hannah wasn't the least bothered about clearing the table, turning her attention instead to the kittens who had woken up from their nap. 'Want to hold them?' she invited, and Kate nodded enthusiastically.

'May I?'

'Of course! Take your pick.'

Unable to resist, she chose two grey kittens that appealed to her, one of which had a tiny white patch on its chest. Cuddling them close, she wished she could take them home. They were so beautiful. She glanced up, embarrassed to find the men had returned and Conor was watching her from the doorway. Her heart skittered as he closed the gap between them, perching on the edge of the table as he helped tease one of the kitten's claws free from her cardigan, cradling the tiny body in the palm of one hand. Kate swallowed and dragged her gaze away.

'Hannah, if you and Nic do decide to rehome some of the

kittens, I'd like to take these two girls when they are old enough to leave,' Conor announced, and Kate's eyes widened in astonishment.

'That's great!' Hannah looked delighted. 'I knew I'd tempt you one day!'

Kate's stomach tightened when Conor looked at her, his smile private and warm. 'I'm tempted. Perhaps you could bring them over in a few weeks.'

'A good idea, my friend,' Nic agreed. 'Then we can see you, Kate and the puppy at the same time, no?'

Conor nodded, moving across the room, and after a final cuddle handed the kitten back to Hannah. 'We'll look forward to it. Now, I'm afraid, we ought to be getting back so we have time to call in to Charlie's and put plan A into action. And if that tin contains some of your coconut and lime cake, please can I take a piece home?' he added with a boyish grin.

As a laughing Nic went off to get the puppy ready for his journey and collect up his toys, food and medication, Hannah shook her head, reaching for a knife and a couple of food bags. 'Conor, you are terrible. Don't you ever think of anything but food?'

'Sometimes.' Kate saw the wicked glint of amusement and hot desire appear in those arresting green eyes. 'Quite often of late.'

She couldn't halt her blush, scared she knew just what he was thinking…because she was thinking it, too. And she shouldn't be. Because it was never going to happen. Not with things the way they were in her life. No matter what Hannah said about him, however seductive his appeal, Conor was not for her.

CHAPTER FIVE

'I CAN'T believe how well that went,' Conor exclaimed with relief. 'For one awful moment I thought it wasn't going to work. Charlie was resistant at first but you were brilliant, Kate, bringing him round,' he praised, glancing at her sitting beside him in the car as they headed back to Glentown-on-Firth at dusk. 'Charlie hasn't been so animated in a long time.'

'The puppy's story affected him,' Kate agreed, and he could hear surprise in her voice, see the appealing glow of pleasure on her face.

It had worked perfectly, the shy little dog and the lonely man who had lost his purpose gravitating towards each other as if each recognised the other's need. As he himself recognised a need in Kate and desperately wanted to take care of her. She hadn't wanted to be drawn into conversation on the journey back from Lochanrig, her attention devoted to the puppy she'd had cradled on the back seat. As much as he longed to talk to her, especially about what had happened during that strange moment in Nic and Hannah's living room, the time wasn't right. Again. It was frustrating but he had to be patient if he wanted to unravel her mysteries and find answers to his ever-growing list of questions about this woman.

'Thank you, Kate.' Parking the car at the surgery, he turned to look at her. 'I've fretted over Charlie for so long.'

'Let's hope it works out. I'm glad he took the puppy or I'd have been horribly tempted myself and it wouldn't be possible for me to have him.'

He heard the wistful note in her voice and smiled. 'Me, too. Have you always loved animals?'

'Yes. There were dogs, cats, guinea pigs and all sorts at home when I was young.'

'You had a good childhood?' he probed gently, welcoming the opportunity to keep her talking about herself.

'Very much so.'

Her reminiscent smile made his stomach turn over. She was so beautiful. And he ached to see her smile more, to hear her laugh, to strip that inner sadness away. He was delighted her home life had been so contented but he couldn't help envying her, too, wishing he had known a settled childhood.

'Where are your family from, Kate?'

'I grew up in Surrey. It's just me and Dad now; he lives in London and is a head teacher. My mum died when I was thirteen.'

'You were an only child?' he chanced, dismayed when he saw her tense, her jaw tightening as she looked away from him.

'No.'

The stiff, cold tone was back and she pushed open the passenger door, sliding out before he had a chance to speak. Hell! OK—so this was another no-go area. He ran the fingers of one hand across his forehead. It was like walking on eggshells around her. If she hadn't been an only child but she described her family as being just her and her father now, what had happened? It was something that upset her, that she was not prepared to talk about and, not wanting to end such a good day on a sour note, he left the car and followed her rigid frame down the path. He could tell she wasn't pleased but she didn't object when he followed her inside and up the stairs to the flat, helping as she silently set about making hot chocolate.

He was no closer to learning what troubled her, which made things very difficult in knowing what to say and how to approach her. She was as skittish as a fawn when things became uncomfortable for her. If she was concerned about being trapped or thrust into some kind of relationship too quickly, he would need to keep things casual, take things slowly, not put any pressure on her. If he told her too soon just how far ahead and how permanently he was thinking, she would run a mile. She would certainly think he was some kind of crazy man if he told her that he had known from the first second that he wanted to spend the rest of his life with her. Hell, he probably was crazy.

Frowning, he ran a hand through his wayward hair. She made him feel things he had never felt before. And everything was so out of his control that it scared him. His whole life had turned inside out the moment he had met her and he wanted more than anything to be with her, to take away her pain, to know her in every way possible.

Patience and care, he told himself, spooning chocolate into the mugs. It went against the grain for him, was contrary to his nature, but if it was what Kate needed, he would keep things light and casual and fun for now. The last thing he wanted was to scare her with serious declarations of undying love, certainly no talk of marriage and a few dozen babies—not yet, anyway.

'It'll be good when Nic and Hannah come over in a few weeks' time,' he commented, cupping his mug in his hands, eager to steer the conversation back to safer ground.

Wary brown eyes looked at him. 'You're serious about having the kittens?'

'Of course I am.' Hoping to engineer another opportunity to spend time with Kate outside work, he voiced a brewing idea. 'Perhaps you'd come to the pet shop with me and help pick out the things I'm going to need.'

'Why did you do that? Offer them a home, I mean,' she asked after a moment and he hoped it was a good sign that she hadn't refused outright.

'I couldn't resist them.' It was pretty impossible to resist her, too, especially when she blew on her drink like that and then licked dusky-rose lips with the tip of her tongue. A groan nearly escaped him. He wanted—needed—to kiss her. His hands tightened round his mug. This was torture. He forced himself to focus, watching her expression as he continued. 'Besides, I could see how much you wanted them.'

The thought that Conor may have decided to rehome the kittens because of her made Kate feel warm inside. 'But I'm not going to be here,' she murmured in confusion, trying to keep up the barriers between them.

'You will be for a while. You can share them.'

She shouldn't even think of agreeing but the lure of the kittens was compelling. 'We'll see.'

'I bet you've thought of names for them, haven't you?' He raised an eyebrow, a twinkle in his eyes. 'I'll tell you mine if you tell me yours.'

She couldn't help but smile. He may confuse her and scare her and challenge her, but he could be irresistible sometimes. 'Willow.'

'Smoky.' He smiled back, his expression so warmly intimate that she couldn't breathe.

It wasn't a good idea to get too involved or close to this man. She had managed to escape from the difficult moment over her family, nearly revealing far too much about herself, terrified Conor was going to pursue the subject and that she would have to talk about Wesley. The aching hole opened up inside her as it always did when she thought about her brother. She missed him so much. Loved him. Was so angry with him. So many emotions jumbled up together. And always the guilt. As ever, the memories threatened to rise up and choke her but she battled against the images, at least while Conor was there. They never left her, invading her sleep every night, affecting every part of her life these last months.

'Are you all right, Kate?'

Conor's husky concern shivered through her. He was too observant, too attuned to her moods. Unable to look at him as she tried to mask her emotions, she nodded. 'I'm fine.' Sensing his hesitation, she held her breath, willing him not to question her further.

'I've really enjoyed today,' Conor commented with obvious sincerity, and she sighed with relief as he turned to wash his mug in the sink before leaving it on the drainer. 'Thank you for the idea and for seeing it through with me.'

'That's OK. It was good meeting Nic and Hannah, I really liked them.' Nervous, she set down her own mug as Conor moved closer and she realised her escape route was blocked.

'They liked you, too. But that's no surprise—you're easy to like.'

Her pulse started racing as her gaze slid inexorably to his and she recognised the burn of desire in his green eyes, fighting against her own response. 'Conor—'

'I know you feel it…' The fingers of one hand tucked some strands of hair behind her ear, lingering to brush against her cheek, making her flesh burn 'This amazing connection between us.'

'Maybe. But I'm adult enough not to act on it.'

'Why?'

She paused, taking a deep breath, desperate not to weaken. 'Look, Conor, I'm only here for a short time.'

'We can take things a day at a time, have some fun,' he suggested, which was exactly what she had expected of him.

The knowledge she had been right and he wanted a temporary diversion enabled her to harden her heart and shore up her fragile resolve. As the pad of his thumb began to trace the swell of her lower lip, she caught his hand and removed it, disconcerted when his fingers closed around hers, preventing her withdrawal, holding her palm against his chest so she could feel the rhythmic beat of his heart. Her body throbbed from his touch, his closeness, the subtle earthy fragrance of him wrapping around her. Part of her wished she was the kind of person to throw caution to the winds and enjoy a few commitment-free nights in his bed. She had no doubt she would enjoy it. But she couldn't do it. Not now. Maybe if Darren had never happened, maybe if the last frightful months had never happened, perhaps then she could have accepted the brief, casual fling Conor was offering, satisfying the yearning ache of want inside her.

But those things *had* happened and for now her life was complicated by so many other issues and problems that this was one step too far, no matter how gorgeous and sexy and tempting Conor was. Meeting his seductive green gaze, she called on all her determination and found the strength to pull her hand free, breaking the electrifying contact.

'I didn't come here for this.'

'What did you come here for, Kate?'

The softly voiced question caught her unawares and she regretted again that Conor saw far more than she wanted him to, understanding and compassion mixing with the desire in his eyes. For a moment she thought of Hannah's story and advice. But her own situation was different and she couldn't take the risk with Conor or open herself up to more hurt.

'I'm just here to work. Adding extra variety to your social life is not part of my job description,' she insisted, wishing she could put more distance between them. Although he wasn't physically touching her, he was far too close, far too tempting.

Amusement sparked in his eyes. 'What do you know about my social life?'

'Nothing.' Cursing the flush that warmed her cheeks at his light-hearted teasing, she looked away from him. 'And that's the way it's going to stay.'

'What about your social life?'

'What about it?' she parried, her discomfort increasing.

'Apart from today, you've done nothing but work this week.'

'I'm here to work, nothing more.'

His head tilted slightly on one side, he looked at her, his expression thoughtful. 'This is a great area, you know. There's lots to see and do. It would be a shame not to enjoy some of it while you're here.'

'Conor—'

'I'd be happy to show you around,' he added with a boyish smile.

She sighed, wondering how long she was going to be able to resist his gentle persistence. 'In the unlikely event I need a tour guide, I'll let you know.' Straightening her shoulders, she forced herself to face him and inject some authority into her voice. 'I don't date colleagues.' Not now, she added silently. A shame she hadn't introduced that rule sooner.

'Will you promise me one thing?'

'What?' Kate asked warily, trembling as his hands skimmed up her arms to her shoulders, moving on to cup her neck and face, his thumbs under her chin forcing her to look at him.

'Don't close your mind to this.'

She tried to ignore the way his touch made her feel all shivery and hot and needy. 'It wouldn't work, Conor.'

'You can't know that.' His voice was husky and persuasive, his eyes sincere. 'Take the time you need, but give us a chance. Please.'

'Conor, I—' She snapped off her words, alarmed how shaky her voice was, fearing he had detected the underlying emotion she had been unable to contain.

Frowning, he tipped up her face, gazing into her eyes. 'Tears, Kate?'

'I don't cry,' she snapped, struggling for control.

'Maybe it's time you did.'

Shocked, she stared at him. 'Why?'

'To get it out.'

'What?'

'Whatever it is that's eating you up inside. Something is haunting you, making you sad,' he clarified, shocking her anew with his frightening perception.

Her hands shook as she caught his wrists, trying unsuccessfully to free herself from his hold. 'I don't know what you mean.'

'Yes, you do.' He stroked her face, his fingers warm, caressing, strong yet exquisitely gentle. 'Let me in, Kate. Tell me what's wrong.'

'Nothing's wrong,' she lied, trying to shore up her battered inner defences, feeling closer to letting go than she had in ages. She had been on the ragged edge for too many weeks but she hadn't cried, terrified that if she ever started she would never stop, that all the pain and grief and horror and guilt suppressed within her would come pouring out and swamp her and she would never be able to cope. She had buried everything inside because that was the only way she could function and go on. She was just a novelty, a diversion, something for Conor to tinker with while she was there, but this was her life and she wasn't strong enough to handle it. Sucking in a ragged breath, she injected some steel into her tone. 'I'm not some project for you to fix, Conor.'

'Is that what you think?' He frowned, hurt and puzzlement in his eyes following her terse comment. 'You're wrong, Kate. I want to help because I care, because I want—' He ceased abruptly, looking uncertain. After a brief hesitation he sighed, closing his eyes for a moment as if struggling for control. When he opened them again they were dark green, warm but troubled. 'I'm not going to hurt you. I'd never do that.'

But he would. Because she knew with utter certainty that she could care for him. Impossibly. Deeply. Irrevocably. That was why he was so dangerous and why she had to stop anything before it started. Physically she wanted him with a desperation that shocked her but emotionally she was too vulnerable. It would hurt too much when the time came for her to walk away. A few nights of pleasure would never be enough with this man. No matter how much he planned not to, he would hurt her—terribly—and she was too fragile to survive any more pain.

Staring into his mesmerising green eyes, dreading to imagine what was showing in her own, she knew she had to send him away. 'Forget about me, Conor.'

'I can't do that.'

'You must,' she whispered, trembling under the touch of his hands on her face, seeing his wry smile.

'It's not humanly possible.'

Scared her heart was going to stop, unable to suck air into her lungs, she stood motionless as he bent his head and pressed a firm but brief kiss to her mouth, releasing her before her body could betray her and respond as every atom of her being craved her to do. He held her gaze for one timeless moment, a welter of emotion and desire churning in the depths of his moss-green eyes, then he turned and walked away, leaving her wanting so much more…and knowing she could never have it.

The days passed quickly and Kate was grateful because being busy gave her little time to brood about her problems…including Conor. Which didn't mean she could put any of them out of her head. Somehow she got through each day and coped with her work, but inside she felt as if she was hanging on by a thread. She was relieved to go out on house visits with the district nurses Jillian, Elaine and Ritchie for a few days, learning more about their regular patients and increasing her knowledge of the area.

By the end of her second week Fred decided she was ready to handle visits on her own and however much she told herself she was thankful, an insidious, traitorous part of her missed Conor's company. When he wasn't flirting with her or trying to get her to go out with him, he was funny and smart and always told her such interesting things about the local history and environment. He also gave her confidence about her work. Shadowing him had been interesting…when she could forget about the man and concentrate on what an amazing doctor he was.

Over two weeks after the visit to Nic and Hannah and seeing the rescued puppy settled with Charlie, Kate had still not been able to put the incident with Conor in her kitchen out of her mind. He remained patiently persistent, somehow managing to give her personal space and yet always be around, lounging in her consulting room at the end of the day, talking about work with his mouth while his eyes said very different things. No matter how hard she tried, how many times she told herself she was doing the right thing, being sensible and thinking of her self-preservation, she couldn't forget that too-short, too-chaste brush of his lips on hers.

Impatient with herself, she parked her car outside the surgery at Thursday lunchtime, using her key to unlock the door as she was running late and the staff had begun their break. She left the tray of patient notes behind Reception to be filed away, then set off along the deserted corridor towards her consulting room. She heard a murmur of voices as she approached Conor's room and she glanced through the open door, pausing in shock as she saw him standing just inside, Jenny in his arms. The young receptionist was clinging to him, her face buried against his chest and one of his hands was stroking her blonde hair. Rooted to the spot, Kate was disturbed by the wave of hurt and disappointment that lanced inside her. He hadn't wasted any time, had he? Only days ago he'd been asking her out, wanting her to give things a chance between them, but it seemed he had moved on. Her heart clenched as she heard some of their conversation.

'I don't know what I'll do,' Jenny murmured in distress.

'Let's wait until the result is back and take it from there,' Conor soothed. 'Whatever happens, I'll be here for you.'

The exchange brought back painful memories. Was something going on between Conor and Jenny? Might Jenny be pregnant? Kate's thoughts turned to Darren and what a fool he had made of her, working his way through a string of junior nurses and doctors behind her back, getting at least one of them pregnant, before she had found him in bed with his latest conquest…a former friend and colleague.

When Conor turned his head and saw her, Kate felt embarrassed at being caught, her heart thudding under her ribs as she met his disapproving green gaze. Looking grim, he moved slightly, reaching out to push his door closed with one foot, shutting her out. She felt rejected and hurt. It wasn't her business what he did. She had wanted him to leave her alone, to turn his attention to someone else, so it was crazy to feel like this because he had.

Once in the sanctuary of her own room, she drew in a steadying breath, unable to concentrate on her paperwork or banish her unease at what she had seen. She wrestled with her thoughts, wondering if she should mention the incident to Fred. But what if she was making too much of it? If she was going to do anything, she needed to know the truth—which meant confronting Conor, asking him to explain what had been going on. Nerves made her tense and uncertain. She would think about it some more. See what happened. Her spirits low, she sighed when her mobile phone rang but brightened when a glance at the display told her the call was from her father in London, who was home from school as the Easter holidays had begun.

'Kate, darling! Is this a bad time?' her father greeted her, his familiar voice tightening her chest with emotion.

'No, it's fine. I've just arrived back from home visits.'

'Are you all right?' She heard his deep-seated concern. 'You sound a bit down.'

'Just a difficult day,' she excused herself.

'How are things going? Are you coping?'

She closed her mind to thoughts of Conor. 'I'm doing all right,' she reassured him, with more conviction than she felt.

They talked for a while and Kate found that hearing his news and talking with him had a calming influence on her inner turmoil.

'I rang because I've planned a little surprise, Kate,' her father announced. 'I thought I'd come up tomorrow and stay for the weekend. Would you like that? Would it be convenient?'

'That would be fantastic! Could you really? I miss you so much!' She laughed, relief and happiness welling inside her. She desperately needed to see him, talk with him. 'Tell me what time your plane arrives and I'll arrange to be there to meet you.'

Chuckling at her enthusiasm, her father gave her the details. 'See you soon, Kate. I love you.'

'I love you, too.'

'I presume there's some reason other than for the pleasure of my company that you've come over here, face like thunder, to raid my fridge and wear a groove in my flooring?' Kyle Sinclair drawled, lounging back in an armchair and taking a pull of his drink.

Scowling, Conor paced up and down Kyle's small living room, tense and moody. It was Friday night and all he had done since the previous afternoon had been to pace and fret and torment himself with dark thoughts.

'For goodness' sake, Conor,' Kyle complained. 'Sit down and talk to me.'

'You don't want to hear about it.'

His friend gave a rough laugh. 'I sure as hell don't want to sit here and watch you walking up and down all evening. You've listened to me moan on about the mess I made of my marriage and the dismal state of my love life for heaven knows how many months. It'll make a change to talk about yours. I assume this is about a woman?' he added with a knowing smile.

Conor paused in his pacing to frown at Kyle. 'What makes you assume a thing like that?'

'Because you're not usually so grumpy and I've never seen you like this before.'

'Bloody women.' Sighing, Conor dropped on to the sofa and picked up his own drink.

'Amen to that,' Kyle agreed with feeling, leaning forward to chink bottles. 'So, what's her name?'

'Kate.'

'Your new locum?'

'Yeah.'

Conor's frown deepened as he thought about the previous afternoon. He had been consoling Jenny when he had seen Kate in the corridor. He'd seen right away she had got the wrong idea about what had been going on and it had ticked him off no end, but he had also been concerned by the paleness of Kate's face and the pain in her huge brown eyes. Unable to leave Jenny, who had needed privacy and time, he had gone along to Kate's consulting room afterwards to find out what was wrong and challenge her about her misjudgement of him, but she had been on the phone, making arrangements for a visit from her father. With a busy afternoon of consultations and clinics, plus a minor emergency coming in, he had been unable to talk with her and things had been strained between them since.

'I just don't understand why she thinks the worst of me and has some warped view of me as some kind of rampant womaniser,' he complained to Kyle, recounting the sorry tale, scared all his hopes and dreams were going to come to nothing and he might never win Kate round. If he didn't, he was going to be the one who ended up with his heart broken.

'You know that's not me. I'm not going to tell her one

moment that I want to spend time with her and then be messing with someone else.' He let out a disgruntled huff of breath. 'The signals Kate's been giving are far from clear but she admitted she felt the connection between us, even if she's wary of acting on it. Whether that's because she's here for a short time or because she's been hurt before I don't know.' He slumped back against the cushions, feeling deflated. 'Anyway, that's why I'm here, as nervous and uncertain as a pathetic adolescent.'

Kyle smiled, his dark blue gaze amused but sympathetic. 'Why don't you do something about it if you care for her so much?'

'Like what?' Conor growled.

'Throw her over your shoulder and whisk her off until she surrenders,' his friend teased, earning himself another scowl.

'I'm not the caveman type. And I don't want to upset her.' He dragged his fingers through his hair in agitation. 'I know something's wrong, Kyle, something bad that's making her hurt inside. She needs gentle handling, not have me charging in like some unfeeling macho idiot. Especially if she already has the wrong impression of me.'

'Talk to her, then.'

Conor sighed, setting down his drink. 'Believe me, I've tried, but I don't get anywhere. There are so many mysteries about Kate and it's so difficult to get close to her. It's like peeling back layers of tissue paper but the image underneath never clears because there are always more and more layers.'

'I hope you're not setting yourself up for trouble, Conor. You said before there were unanswered questions about her CV and why she was working with you. Are you really sure about her?' Kyle fretted, leaning forward and resting his elbows on his knees.

'I've never felt like this before, Kyle, but I just know Kate's the one for me. Whether I can ever convince her of that is another matter,' he admitted, voicing his inner fears.

'I'm hardly qualified to give advice when it comes to relationships after the way I've screwed up mine.' Kyle took another drink, a frown on his face. 'But if you feel this strongly, follow your heart. Just be careful. Please. I don't want to see you get hurt, Conor.'

'Kate's an excellent doctor—although she doesn't believe in herself right now—and the patients love her.' Hell, he loved her, but he wasn't confessing that aloud, not while he was so wary of his ground and of ever winning Kate's trust. 'She's smart and kind and she has a true natural beauty. But something is hurting inside her. I can't find out what it is but I can see the building tension and panic in her eyes. She's trying hard to fight it but it's as if she's hanging onto her control like a climber without a safety rope who's gripping the only available hand hold with her fingertips and is starting to slip. I'm scared for her, Kyle. What's going to happen to her when that inevitable fall comes?'

'You be there to catch her, buddy, and you hang on tight.'

'I plan to—' he looked up, meeting his friend's understanding dark blue gaze '—if she'll let me.'

CHAPTER SIX

KATE looked at the surly teenager slumped on the chair by her desk and smothered a sigh. Fred had offered to switch Saturday surgery with her, knowing of her weekend visitor, but she had declined, anxious to pull her weight and having taken the previous afternoon off to collect her father from Prestwick airport. It had been wonderful to see him. This morning he was content to wander along the seafront and explore the village while she worked, but faced with Lindsay Graham and her mother she was beginning to wish she had accepted Fred's offer after all.

Her list had included two patients with gastroenteritis, one with angina, one with allergic rhinitis, one sent to hospital with suspected appendicitis, a baby with earache and a young man suffering the after-effects of a binge-drinking night out, which had resulted in him falling off the sea wall, grazing his face, spraining his wrist and bruising his ego. She had been unable to cure the latter symptom but had recommended a more modest consumption rate and some self-control in future. Self-control made her think of Conor, which was not a good idea, given how close her own was to slipping where he was concerned, even though she had yet to solve the Jenny issue, which had given her two sleepless nights so far. She pushed the thoughts aside and concentrated on the glowering teenager and her over-anxious mother.

'Mrs Graham,' she began again, summoning her patience and resisting the temptation to call for reinforcements. 'I think it would be better if you waited outside while I see Lindsay.'

'But she's my daughter, she's only fourteen! She doesn't have secrets from me,' the woman wailed, and Kate glanced at Lindsay who rolled her eyes as only a teenager could, willing to bet there were all manner of secrets between mother and daughter. 'It's my right to be here.'

'It's my right to some privacy and I don't want you here,' Lindsay riposted rudely.

Rising to her feet, Kate rounded the desk, her tone placating. 'This isn't getting us anywhere, is it? Mrs Graham, please, will you sit in the waiting room for a short while? I'll call you back in when we're ready.'

Kate accompanied the reluctant Sara Graham to Reception where Aileen took charge, assessing the situation at once and organising a cup of coffee for the nervy mother, sitting her down with some magazines so Kate could escape back to her consulting room to face the difficult teenager.

'OK, Lindsay,' she began. 'Let's start again. Can you tell me how you are feeling?'

The girl gave a nonchalant shrug. 'I just feel off-colour. Achy and low. And I've had a sore throat for a while.'

'Is it all right if I check you over?'

'S'pose,' she agreed uncooperatively.

Kate carried out her examination, finding that the glands in Lindsay's neck were a little enlarged and tender. Her throat was inflamed but not infected, and there were characteristic petechiae or small reddish-purple spots in the mouth, which helped confirm her suspicions on the cause of the teenager's problems.

'Has swallowing been painful, Lindsay?'

Again the disinterested shrug. 'It's sore but it hasn't stopped me eating or talking.'

'And you've had some pain? Does that include headaches?'

'Yes,' the girl agreed.

Kate nodded. 'Have you felt feverish at all?'

'A bit. Yes. I'm so tired and haven't any energy to do anything. What do you think it is?'

'I suspect you have glandular fever, Lindsay. I'm sure you feel quite weak and achy but that will pass,' Kate reassured her. The girl's symptoms were fairly moderate and she had detected no enlargement or tenderness of the spleen. 'I need to take some blood to be tested to ensure nothing else is going on.'

Lindsay remained quiet as Kate did a few more routine checks, taking the blood sample before drawing off her gloves and returning to her desk. She was about to explain what Lindsay needed to do when the phone rang.

'Excuse me a moment, Lindsay,' she apologised.

'Kate, I'm sorry,' Aileen said when she answered the phone. 'Conor's here and has calmed Sara Graham down, but she's anxious to return to her daughter.'

'Just a moment.' Kate put her hand over the mouthpiece and looked at Lindsay. 'Do you mind if your mother comes back now we've finished the examination?' She took the half-hearted nod as agreement. 'All right, Aileen. Thank you.'

Sara Graham arrived, with Conor following. Wondering why he was there on his Saturday off, Kate met his gaze, seeing his sympathetic smile, knowing he understood and was waiting to see if there was anything he could do. Rather than seeing it as interference, Kate welcomed the back-up, even if she was very aware of him.

'Sit down, please, Mrs Graham,' Kate said.

'What's the matter with Lindsay?'

'It's nothing very serious,' she said soothingly. 'Lindsay has glandular fever and—'

'But that's the kissing disease, isn't it?' The woman's eyes widened and she swung round to engage her daughter. 'What have you been doing, Lindsay? Have you been seeing a boy?'

Lindsay slouched on the chair. 'Mother, you are so ridiculous.'

'That's only one of the ways of catching it,' Kate intervened, keen to prevent another family dispute.

'See.' Lindsay smirked at her mother. 'Don't you know anything?'

'But, Lindsay!' Mrs Graham fretted.

Conor stepped forward and Kate nodded as he raised a querying eyebrow, welcoming his help. 'Sara, this isn't relevant. Why not let Kate explain what help Lindsay needs now?'

'All right.' The woman glanced up at Conor with a tremulous smile. 'If you think so.'

'Daddy said she only insisted on bringing me so she could flutter her eyelashes at you, Dr Anderson.'

Mrs Graham flushed and turned to remonstrate with her daughter. Kate tried not to look at Conor but couldn't help it, seeing him make a face behind Mrs Graham's back, doing an impossibly good impression of Lindsay rolling her eyes. She looked away, managing to turn her burst of laughter into a smothered cough. The man was outrageous. Clearing her throat, she focused on the notes, composing herself before returning her attention to her patient, trying to ignore Conor's distracting presence.

'Mrs Graham, we'll test the blood sample to ensure there is nothing else. For now Lindsay needs lots of rest and plenty of fluids. I'll prescribe paracetamol for the aches and temperature.'

'What about antibiotics?' the woman fussed.

'Glandular fever is caused by a virus, Mrs Graham. Antibiotics don't kill viruses, they help treat bacterial infections.'

Mrs Graham turned to look at Conor. 'Is that right?'

'Exactly as Kate told you,' he replied, and Kate appreciated the way he insisted the woman take note of her own opinion and not keep questioning him.

'But Lindsay could be ill for months with glandular fever, couldn't she?' Sara fretted. 'What will we do?'

Unable to prevent a glance towards Conor, she warmed at the encouragement in his eyes. 'Most people recover in a few weeks and do not go on to have complications. Lindsay will feel tired during that time, and maybe for a short while afterwards, but she should soon show signs of improvement.' Kate turned to the sulky teenager. 'Lindsay, you must drink plenty of fluids and rest. No rough or contact sports for at least a couple of months. You should both know that it is advisable not to share towels, cups and so on and...' She paused, daring another look at Conor for support, anxious not to spark off another mother/daughter row. 'Avoid close contact and kissing.'

'We need to discuss that,' Mrs Graham stated.

Lindsay rolled her eyes again. 'Mother.'

'Close contact and kissing also means with family and friends,' Conor clarified, hopefully excavating them from another difficult moment.

Kate smiled and rose to her feet, eager to end the torturous consultation. 'Come back and see me in ten days, Lindsay. We'll assess how you feel then, and we'll have the result of your blood test. If you feel worse in the meantime or want anything explained, phone me or come to the surgery,' she added, handing over the paracetamol prescription.

Thankful that Conor followed the Grahams down the corridor to Reception to see them out, Kate sat down and phoned through to Aileen. 'Is that it or do I have anyone else to see?'

'No, pet,' the practice manager reassured her. 'You get yourself home and enjoy your weekend. Tom is here, waiting to take you to lunch.'

'Thanks, Aileen.'

Eager to see her father, she wrote up her notes, logged off her computer and left the room.

* * *

Conor held the door open for Sara and Lindsay Graham, thankful when they took their leave. Poor Kate! Things might be tense between them but at least he'd made her laugh. Smiling, he turned towards the reception desk and saw that Aileen was talking with a distinguished-looking man he didn't recognise. Dark-haired and dressed in casual but smart clothes, the man was tall and trim.

Aileen smiled and beckoned him over. 'Have you met Kate's father?'

Interested, Conor walked across to join them just as Kate came along the corridor. Her smile faltered as she saw them together and Conor's curiosity increased. He waited in silence as Tom enveloped her in a hug, admitting to himself that he had popped in to return some notes, after being called out in the early hours, on the off chance there might be an opportunity to meet Tom Fisher.

'Hello, darling. I gather you've had a busy morning.'

'It's been quite eventful.' Kate drew back and Conor noted her wary expression as she glanced at him. 'Thanks for your help with the Grahams.'

'No problem.'

She looked uncomfortable, stepping closer to her father as if for comfort or protection. Either way, Conor didn't like it. 'Have you been introduced, Dad?'

'Not yet.' Her father smiled, the expression in his brown eyes, so like Kate's, curious and open. 'We were just about to take care of that when you joined us.'

'This is Dr Conor Anderson. He's one of the partners here at the Solway.'

'Delighted to meet you.' Tom smiled, holding out his hand.

Conor shook it, aware of Kate's nervousness. 'Hello, Mr Fisher. It's good you could visit. I hope you enjoy your stay in Glentown.'

'Tom, please. And, thank you, I'm sure I shall have a

lovely time.' Tom turned to Kate and rested an arm around her shoulders. 'My daughter settling in all right?'

'Kate's doing very well. We're lucky to have her with us,' Conor replied, meeting her anxious gaze with a smile.

'Good, good. It's a relief to know she's making friends.' The accompanying smile included Aileen. 'Perhaps you'd care to join us for lunch? We're having a snack at the local pub before going to explore St Ninian's Cave while the weather holds.'

'Dad, I'm sure Conor has other plans.'

Kate's rush to dismiss him brought out his stubborn streak. 'Not at all. I'd be delighted to accept,' he agreed, seeing Kate's expression close.

'Splendid!' The older man turned to Aileen. 'Would you be free to come, too, my dear?'

'Well, I— That's very kind of you,' Aileen murmured, clearly flustered, her freckled cheeks pinkening.

Conor glanced at Kate, pleased that she was more amused than upset by her father's interest in Aileen. He wished he could invite them all to his house for a meal, not having had the chance to take Kate there yet, but he held back, knowing Kate would want to spend time alone with her father that weekend. As they waited for Aileen to collect her things, Conor saw Kate murmuring to her father. He met Tom's gaze and saw the older man's puzzled expression. What had she said?

If he hoped to learn more about Kate's mysterious past over lunch, he was disappointed. They had an enjoyable time but there was no opportunity to steer the conversation towards more personal topics. Tom was warm and funny—it was easy to see where Kate had acquired her intelligence and kindness of spirit—and Conor took to the man straight away, finding someone who shared his interest in the environment and who was keen to learn about local history. Kate seemed on edge throughout their meal and he wondered if she was scared her father would let something slip. Frustration gnawed at him. He still didn't know what the problems were and what Kate was hiding.

When they'd finished their lunch and left the pub, Tom took his arm, allowing the two women to walk on ahead. 'A quiet word?'

'Of course. Is something wrong?' Conor asked, seeing worry cloud the older man's eyes.

'I can see you care about my daughter,' Tom murmured, his gaze following Kate as she talked with Aileen. 'Conor, look after Kate for me.'

'I plan to,' he said, his own concern for her increasing with her father's obvious anxiety.

The man nodded, understanding in his eyes. Conor wanted to ask more about what was going on and why Tom was worried but Kate turned at that moment, looking nervous when she saw them talking together. Saying no more, Tom moved across to join her and, as the pair set off to the Isle of Whithorn to explore the historic site of St Ninian's Cave, Conor walked Aileen home.

'You really care about Kate, don't you?'

Surprised and alarmed at Aileen's perception, Conor glanced at her, about to deny it, then changed his mind. 'Yes, I do.'

'There'll be mourning across the county when you settle down,' Aileen predicted with an affectionate smile, slipping her arm through his. 'I think Kate needs you, Conor. You'd be good together. I hope it works out.'

'Thanks, Aileen. So do I. You seem taken with Tom, if I may say so,' he teased, laughing as Aileen's cheeks flushed with warmth again.

'Isn't it foolish, at my age?'

'Age has nothing to do with it and you have a lot of living ahead of you. You deserve to be happy—Craig would have wanted that.' He had spent many hours helping Aileen through her grief after her husband had been lost at sea while out on a hazardous RNLI rescue five years previously. 'It's time you had someone new in your life. And Tom's a really nice man.'

Aileen looked up at him with a watery smile. 'He is, isn't he? Like father, like daughter, it seems. I'll have to get my matchmaking hat on and give you and Kate a helping hand!'

'You don't think I'm capable of winning her round?' The joking tone hid his inner concern that Kate would never return his feelings.

'If anyone can, it's you.' Aileen's smile was rueful. 'I was thinking that if Kate stayed on here, there would be more chance of Tom visiting.'

'An ulterior motive if ever I heard one!' He waited while she found her front door key and unlocked the door, bending to drop a kiss on her cheek. 'I'd be delighted if things developed for you and Tom, Aileen, but I'll do my own wooing, thanks.'

As Conor headed home, he reflected on the impact the Fisher family had made on the inhabitants of Glentown-on-Firth. He only hoped, despite his nervousness and misgivings, that the outcome for them all would be a happy one.

Monday morning arrived too soon. Kate felt bereft with her father gone, although their final talk before his flight had left her unsettled. The conversation replayed itself in her head as she prepared for work.

'It's been wonderful spending this time with you, Kate.'

'Come up whenever you can,' she said with a smile, hoping to see him often.

Uncertainty shadowed his eyes. 'Would you mind if I kept in touch with Aileen?'

'Of course not.' Her smile widened to a grin. 'I thought you were getting on well!'

'She's a delightful lady. I've left a little something, if you wouldn't mind delivering it.'

'No problem!'

'Your Conor seems a lovely young man,' her father teased. Kate tensed, her smile fading. 'He's not "my" Conor.'

'I'm sure he'd like to be! He's very smitten with you.'

'I don't think so, Dad.' She cursed the warmth that flushed her cheeks. 'We work together. That's all. He's a good doctor but he's just like Darren, stringing along half the women in the district.'

Her father frowned, the look in his eyes speculative as he watched her. 'Conor didn't strike me as being remotely like Darren. Far from it. I found Conor sincere and caring. Are you not using that as an excuse to prevent him getting close to you?'

Her blush deepened. 'I'm only here for a short time. It wouldn't work.'

'Nonsense. The change in you this last month has been remarkable. You've lost that pallor and you've put some weight back on. What we need now is something to put a sparkle back in your eyes.'

'I'm fine.'

His smile was sad but resigned. 'We both know that isn't true, darling. You've never talked about what happened—and you told me on Saturday not to mention it, that no one here knows anything, not even about Wesley. Do you think that's healthy?'

'There's no need for them to know anything.' She sucked in a deep breath. 'I'm here because I need to know if I can still be a doctor.'

'You're an excellent doctor. Remember the lives you saved, Kate.'

For a moment she closed her eyes, but the mental images of those lives she had not saved were too vivid and she opened them again. 'But it wasn't enough. And now I'm running away.'

'You're not running,' her father scolded, his frown deepening.

She shook her head, denying the comfort. 'What would you call it?'

'Recovering. Moving on. Being human.' His hand cupped her cheek, lingering sadness in his eyes and pain in his voice. 'Don't let this rule the rest of your life, Kate. I don't want to lose you, too.'

'I'm sorry, Dad.'

'It's not your fault, darling. None of it is. Please, believe that.' He drew her into his arms, hugging her tight. 'I love you.'

She hugged him back. 'I love you, too.'

All her life he had been there for her, picking her up when she had fallen or when she had broken up with a boy-friend. But a sticking plaster and some soothing words wouldn't help fix this.

'James was right—this place is good for you. Open yourself up, Kate, let people get close to you. There's nothing to say you couldn't stay here if you wanted to.' Hugging her one last time, he stepped back. 'Whatever you choose, I'll always be here for you.'

By 'people' her father had meant Conor, she knew, and his parting advice nagged at her. Was he right? Was she making excuses to keep Conor at bay? She was uncertain of him and his motives, and she was too fragile for a temporary fling, unable to handle the inevitable pain that would follow. She had enough worries, getting her career back on track and facing all the demons she held so tightly inside. Frowning, she left the flat and walked round to the surgery, finding Aileen at Reception.

'Oh, my goodness!' The older woman flushed as Kate handed her the plant and card from her father. 'How sweet of him.'

'Dad was very taken with you.' She smiled, wondering if anything would come of the friendship.

'Would it be all right…? I mean, would you mind if I sent a note to thank him?'

Amused that the efficient practice manager looked as flustered as a teenager, Kate shook her head. 'Of course not. Dad devoted himself to family and work after my mother died. He has many hobbies and friends, but he's never been interested in another woman before. I'd be delighted for him if he found happiness—and for you.'

'Thank you. You're a lovely lassie.' Aileen's eyes glittered. 'I'll put the plant in the staffroom before the rush starts.'

Left alone, Kate was checking some mail when Jenny took her place at Reception, her face pale, her eyes red-rimmed. Concerned, Kate was wondering whether to intervene when Conor arrived, his green gaze meeting hers.

'Hi.'

'Morning,' she managed, wondering how one word delivered in that husky tone and soft accent could make her shiver with awareness.

'Good weekend?'

'Lovely.'

He nodded, his attention switching to Jenny. 'All right, sweetie?'

'I'm OK.' Jenny found a semblance of a smile for him.

Leaning over the desk, he stroked her cheek with his fingers. 'Good girl. I'll see you later.'

'Eleven-thirty?'

'No problem.'

Picking up his note tray, he headed to his room. Disturbed, Kate collected her own notes and as patients began arriving she followed down the corridor, pausing at Conor's open door.

'Everything all right?'

He glanced up, his green eyes cool. 'Fine, thanks. You?'

'I suppose. I…'

'What?'

She sucked in a breath, nervous about confronting him. 'About Jenny.'

'What about her?' He leaned back in his chair and linked his hands behind his head, the action tightening his T-shirt across the muscled contours of his chest.

'I just wondered if it was…appropriate,' she murmured, feeling foolish.

'Appropriate?'

He sounded more amused than annoyed. 'Do you always—?' She broke off. 'Manhandle' was a bit too strong a word and she searched in vain for something else to say.

'Do I always what, Kate?' he challenged, the amusement fading. 'Jenny is a valued member of staff and a friend.'

'And that's how you behave with your staff?'

'If they are upset and in need of a cuddle, yes.' He leaned forward and rested his forearms on his desk. 'You have some problem with that?'

Kate bit her lip, wishing she had never started this appalling conversation. Why should she care a jot what the wretched man did and with whom he did it? 'No, no problem,' she lied.

'Good.' He paused, enigmatic green eyes darkening, holding her captive. 'Perhaps you'd like to try it some time.'

It was clear what he meant and the suggestiveness in his voice made a knot of longing tighten in her stomach. 'No, thanks.'

Her hackles rose as she heard him chuckle and she continued down the corridor, slamming her bag and notes on her desk. Damn the man. He thought far too much of himself. And she was still unsettled about the Jenny thing. Was it perfectly innocent? Was she just over-sensitive about anything that smacked of impropriety because of Darren?

Throughout a long and varied morning surgery, Conor refused to let his preoccupation detract from his care of his patients, but he was concerned and puzzled about Kate, as well as anxious about his eleven-thirty appointment. He hadn't received the phone call he had been expecting when, his consultations having overrun by thirty minutes, his final patient arrived.

'I've decided to come in on my own if that's all right,' the blond-haired young man commented, closing the door behind him.

'Of course, Mark.' Conor smiled, gesturing towards a chair. 'I've not heard from the hospital yet but I'll ring now you are here. They promised your results would be ready this morning. How have things been this last week?'

'A bit gruesome, to be honest,' he admitted with a grimace, his hands clenched.

Conor nodded sympathetically. 'It must be difficult. Let's hope we can put your worries to rest now.'

Waiting to be connected to the right department at the hospital, he tried to imagine how he would have felt at twenty-four, his whole life ahead of him, moving in with his childhood sweetheart and suddenly finding a testicular lump, immediately thinking the worst. He hadn't wanted to give Mark false hope but, having examined him before fasttracking him to the hospital, he was as confident as he could be that it was not cancer. The ultrasound could confirm his hunch that Mark had either an inguinoscrotal hernia or an epididymal cyst. Smiling his encouragement as the call was answered, he prayed his instinct was right.

'I don't believe it,' Mark murmured for the hundredth time, and Conor smiled as he walked him to the door.

'I'm going to the staffroom to have a drink before my house calls. Come and get me if you want me to explain anything again.'

Looking bemused, Mark nodded. 'Thanks, Conor.'

Relieved the confirmation had come through and Mark's diagnosis was an inguinal hernia in the scrotum, Conor headed for the staffroom, finding Kate and a couple of the nurses there.

'Hi.' He noted how Kate's wary brown gaze skittered away from him. 'Busy morning?'

'The usual. You?' she asked after a pause, looking even more restless as Kristen and Sandra pulled on their coats and headed out for lunch, leaving them alone.

'Busy but good.' He prepared his hot chocolate and turned to watch her. 'Kate, I want to—'

'Conor?'

He saw Kate tense as Jenny's voice reached them. 'In here,' he answered, setting his mug aside just in time as the young receptionist rushed into the room and flung herself into his arms. Delighted for Jenny but frustrated at yet another interruption when he had hoped to talk with Kate, he smiled as Mark appeared in the staffroom doorway.

'We can't thank you enough, Conor.' Jenny smiled through her tears as she hugged him.

'I told you it would be all right.' He let her go and glanced at Kate, who was watching in confusion as Jenny moved back to Mark and wrapped her arms around him. 'I'm delighted for you both.'

'It's definitely not a tumour?' Jenny said, her anxious gaze flicking between them.

Conor was swift to reassure her. 'Definitely not. Mark will need an operation to surgically repair the hernia but that's all.'

'You've been brilliant,' Mark said as Jenny sagged against him. 'It's been a hellish week. Jenny's told me what a support you have been to her.'

Conor risked another glance at Kate who had risen to her feet and was quietly slipping on her coat. 'That's what friends are for.'

'Finding the lump gave us such a scare and I don't know what we would have done if you hadn't helped. It's made us realise how short time could be and what is important.' Blushing, Jenny smiled up at him. 'Mark and I have decided to get married in the summer and start a family as soon as possible.'

'Just be happy—you both deserve it.'

His enjoyment in his friends' news was dampened when Kate slipped out of the room. He wanted to follow her, talk to her, discover what was hurting her, ask why she'd misjudged him, but rudeness prevented him deserting Jenny and Mark, who still had questions for him. But some time soon he was determined to engineer time alone with Kate to try and get closer to her. Her father's words came back to him, the request he take care of Kate. He planned to, but he wished he knew what it was that she needed protecting from, what had happened to cause her such inner hurt and turmoil.

CHAPTER SEVEN

WITH Fred taking a few days off, the rest of the week was frantic. Kate was relieved as it helped her avoid Conor and allowed little time for him to continue his habit of lounging in her consulting room at the end of the day for a chat. She felt guilty about the Jenny situation, having allowed her own past experience and the rumours she had heard about Conor to mistrust him and wrongly judge him. She had been touched by the scene she had witnessed in the staffroom. There were many more depths to Conor than she would have expected. His care of his patients, staff and friends was beyond compare and he gave selflessly of himself. The more she came to know him the less like Darren he seemed, both as a doctor and a person, but that only made her more edgy because it was becoming harder to keep up her barriers and hold Conor at a distance.

As her final patient of Friday morning arrived, Kate noticed that the large young woman who entered the room and closed the door appeared exceptionally nervous and was shaking with fright. Short platinum curls framed a round, attractive face but her skin was very pale and her dove-grey eyes were wide with anxiety. She sat down with obvious re-luctance and Kate glanced at the notes. Louise Kerr was twenty-two and rarely visited the surgery. The last notation was from two years ago, written by a Dr Myers, and Kate felt anger burning inside her at the comment written in a tight, neat hand. 'Told patient she was disgustingly obese and not to come back until she lost weight.' Smothering a curse, she pushed aside her fury and disbelief, focusing on the trembling young woman.

'Hi,' she said with a smile, keeping things friendly. 'May I call you Louise?'

'F-fine.'

'Good to see you, Louise. I'm Kate. How can I help you today?'

The young woman shredded a paper tissue in her fingers. 'I didn't want to come, only my friend Julie MacIntyre—you saw her little boy Dominic recently—said how nice you were. I'm sorry to bother you but the pain is getting worse,' she confided after a long pause, the whispered words so soft Kate had to strain to hear her.

'You are not being a bother, Louise,' she said reassuringly, although if the single line in the notes from her previous visit was any indication of the reception the poor girl had received last time she had sought help, it was not surprising she was so scared. 'You are as valuable and deserving as any other patient and I'm here to do all I can to help.'

Fearful grey eyes widened in surprise. 'I— The last doctor I saw here…' Her fingers resumed the shredding as her words trailed off.

'Go on,' Kate encouraged.

'Dr Myers. She said all that was the matter with me was that I was so fat and I was just wasting her time.'

Kate wanted to hit something. Preferably Dr Myers. She sucked in a breath and tried to cool her temper. 'I'm very sorry that Dr Myers failed you, Louise, it must have been a horrible experience being treated so badly and not taken seriously. Did you not feel able to talk to Dr Murdoch or Dr Anderson?'

'Oh, no! Dr Murdoch is a friend of my parents, I've

known him all my life, and I couldn't possibly see Conor—Dr Anderson.'

A flush stained Louise's cheeks and Kate frowned again. From all she had discovered of his skills as a doctor she couldn't believe Conor had been lacking in tact and understanding, too. Before she could voice her concern, Louise continued.

'I mean, Conor's always so wonderfully kind but I'd be far too embarrassed to let him see me. He's so gorgeous,' she confided, displaying all the signs of a smitten female. 'I couldn't talk to him about that sort of thing and definitely never take my clothes off and let him see how revolting I am.'

'Louise, you are a human being, a lovely young lady, and we are here to help you.'

Tears shimmered in her eyes. 'I don't like to waste your time.'

'You are not wasting my time. I can see from your notes that you aren't someone who makes a fuss and you don't seek the help you are entitled to. But you're back today. That's good. It must have been hard for you to come,' she said, working to set the anxious girl at her ease and gain some trust. 'Let's try and make a new start. Begin at the beginning. All right?'

Louise nodded and bit her lip, tears spiking her lashes. As Kate encouraged her to talk, years of bullying, shame and fear poured out along with the health problems, and Kate struggled to keep an upwelling of emotion in check.

'I've tried every diet imaginable, tried exercising, but I'm laughed at if I go to the gym and nothing works long term, more just goes back on again if I lose any weight. It's like a vicious circle. And the more problems I have with my health, the more people taunt me, the less motivation there is.'

'OK.' Kate blew out a breath, her mind sorting out all the issues here. 'Let's deal with one thing at a time. You have problems with your periods?'

Blushing, Louise lowered her gaze and nodded. 'They are

irregular but when I do have one it's very heavy and lasts ages. And the breaks between are getting shorter and shorter. I never know what is going to happen or when, but when it starts, it's just awful. It's got so bad I can't hold down a job and I can't leave the house for days sometimes.'

'Do you have any pain with them?'

'I have pelvic pain most of the time,' Louise admitted, her voice a little stronger as she talked. 'It's hard to describe but I feel it deep inside, all around the pelvis and through my lower back.'

Kate nodded, making notes. 'And is that the pain you mentioned earlier, the pain that has become so bad you were brave enough to come here today?'

'No,' Louise admitted, lowering her gaze.

'Tell me about this other pain, Louise.'

As she ran through the symptoms, her eating patterns and the times of pain, the more Kate suspected gallstones. Louise was very young but all the signs were there. There was so much going on she wasn't sure where to begin.

'Is it all right if I do a few checks, Louise? I'd like to test your blood pressure,' she explained, taking things one step at a time so as not to alarm her, careful not to cause embarrassment as she substituted a larger cuff to fit Louise's arm. There were no previous readings to compare with but Kate was concerned that the level was on the high side and made a note to keep a regular watch on Louise's BP over the coming months. She checked the girl's eyes, unsurprised to find the conjunctivae pale. 'Is it all right if I take a blood sample?'

'Why do you need to do that?'

'Losing so much blood could make you anaemic and that would make you feel low and tired. A simple test will confirm it and a course of iron tablets will help. I want to check your hormone levels, see if something there is adding to the problems with your periods,' she explained, preparing what she needed, making a mental note to check thyroid function, too.

'All right,' Louise agreed.

'Thank you.' She set about taking the blood sample and smiled as she finished up. 'All done. You are doing really well, Louise. I'd also like you to provide a urine sample for me. No hurry right now, but I'll give you a sample bottle and you can drop it in when you can. I need that because I want to ensure there is nothing there that we don't know about,' she explained, thinking about any signs of diabetes.

'OK.'

Knowing this was going to be difficult, she tackled the next problem. 'I don't want to rush you, but I would like to examine you, Louise, so I can help find out what's making you so uncomfortable. Will you let me do that?'

'I don't know if I can.' The words were whispered, the grey eyes filling with tears once more. 'Do I h-have to?'

'I would never make you do anything against your will, Louise, but we need to sort out this pain. I'm not going to think anything and I'm definitely not judging you. I just want to help. Please?'

When Louise finally agreed, Kate kept things as business-like and dignified as she could so as not to cause more stress than necessary, leaving any question of an internal exam for when Louise was more trusting and relaxed. Keeping a blanket drawn up to Louise's waist, Kate felt her abdomen, finding tenderness in the upper-right quadrant. It was true that Louise's shape made it hard to feel but, combined with the other reported symptoms, she was pretty certain of her diagnosis.

'OK, Louise, you've been great. You can straighten your clothes now and sit down when you are ready.' Kate gave her some space and returned to her desk, jotting notes as she waited for Louise to rejoin her. 'Now, then, one thing at a time. We'll test for the anaemia and hormone levels, plus monitor your thyroid activity, and I'll check the urine sample as soon as you provide it,' she said, handing over the sample pack which the young woman slipped into her bag. 'While we wait for the test results I'm going to start you on a course of iron tablets and I'll write you a prescription for a low-dose contraceptive pill and we'll use it temporarily to begin to get your periods under control.'

'What could be making them bad?'

'I'm not sure yet.' Kate smiled in reassurance, anxious not to worry Louise until they knew more but considering the possibility of endometriosis or fibroids. 'When we have a clearer idea what's going on, we'll probably change you to a different medication but we'll wait for the results and see how the Pill helps you in the short term.'

'Gosh,' Louise murmured, tucking the prescription into her bag to join the sample pack.

'I know, it's a lot to take in.' Kate gave her a moment to absorb what she had heard. 'Now, about your upper abdominal pain, nausea and so on. I think you might have gallstones, Louise. It's a horrible pain, but we can do something about it. I do need to refer you to the hospital, though, to have a scan.'

Grey eyes widened in alarm. 'Oh, I can't do that!'

'It's painless, Louise. They just put some gel on your skin and the ultrasound can look inside and see if you have the stones or not.'

'It's not that. I—'

As the young woman broke off, Kate nodded, understanding her fear of being examined. 'I'll contact them myself and explain the situation, I promise.'

'And if I do have these stones?' she said after several moments.

'We'll cross that bridge if and when we come to it. The important thing now is to know what we are dealing with.'

Louise nodded, her fingers twisting together in agitation. 'I'll try.'

'Good girl. In the meantime, there are things you can do about the attacks of pain. With gallstones, it helps if you cut out fatty foods because they aggravates the condition. I'll give you a leaflet about it. Anything you can do to remove trigger foods will make a difference to the pain.'

'Really?'

Kate smiled at Louise's surprise. 'Really. I want you to take one iron tablet three times a day—they might make you a bit constipated so make sure you eat plenty of fibre while you are taking them and lots of vitamin C, which helps your body absorb the iron. Eat plenty of fruit and vegetables, whole grains, white meat, fish, and cut back all you can on dairy products and fatty foods,' she advised, handing over the leaflet.

'I'll do that.'

'Is there anything you want to ask me, Louise?'

Frowning in consideration, she shook her head. 'No. I don't think so.'

'OK, we'll leave it there today. You've done really well, Louise, I'm so glad you came to see me. Things will get better, I promise.'

'I don't know what to say,' the young woman whispered. 'You've been so kind, I never expected...'

'You have every right to expect. I want you to come and see me again in a week, but if you have any concerns in the meantime or any pain that worries you, just call me. And you'll drop that sample in for me?' Kate stressed, walking with Louise to the deserted reception area.

'I will. Thank you so much.'

Kate gave her shoulder a gentle squeeze. 'It's no problem, honestly.'

Surprised how late it was and discovering everyone had gone to lunch, Kate unlocked the front door, seeing Conor approaching from the car park.

'Hi, Louise,' he said. 'We haven't seen you for a while. Everything all right?'

Kate noticed Louise blush scarlet at Conor's attention and warm smile.

'Yes, thank you. Kate's been lovely.'

'That's good.'

She almost flushed herself at the approval and slow burn of heat in Conor's green eyes as his gaze met hers before he walked on into the building. Pulling herself together, she held the door open for Louise. 'I'll see you soon.'

She watched the young woman walk away, head down, shoulders hunched. There would be a lot of work ahead on all kinds of issues and she wanted to ensure that Louise would be able to seek help from one of the other doctors when she herself was no longer there. Frowning at the welter of emotions churning inside her at the thought of leaving Glentown-on-Firth, she locked the door and returned to her consulting room, staring down at her notes, her chin resting in her hands. She was seething with fury at the treatment Louise had experienced in the past, shocked at the lack of care and understanding demonstrated by Dr Myers.

A brief tap on the door was the only warning she received before Conor came in. She was amazed when he handed her a pack of sandwiches and a fresh fruit smoothie.

Disconcerted, she met his gaze. 'What's this for?'

'You missed lunch.'

'I can't stop now,' she said, unsettled by his thoughtfulness. 'I have a couple of house calls to catch up on before after-noon surgery.'

'I've done them.'

To her chagrin, he sat himself on her desk, far too close, far too familiar. 'You have?'

'Mmm.' Feeling him assessing her, she concentrated on the refreshing tangy drink. 'It was clear you needed time—Louise was here over an hour—so I did the calls.'

'I'm sorry,' she responded, unable to keep the stiffness from her voice.

'There's nothing to apologise for, it wasn't a criticism,' he said, his voice warm and concerned. 'You gave Louise what she needed.' He paused and she couldn't stop herself looking up at him, his nearness making her pulse race. 'So, what's the story? Everything all right with Louise?'

'Yes,' she lied. Green eyes studied her as he waited and she sighed. 'Sort of. Why?'

'What's wrong?'

Did the wretched man always have to read her so easily, know what she was thinking? She shook her head in denial but he wasn't buying it.

'Kate, talk to me.'

'What was Dr Myers like?'

Conor let out an exclamation of surprise. 'I've not heard her name mentioned in a while.'

'And?'

'She was hopeless,' he admitted, frustration evident in his tone as he folded his arms across his chest. 'Well qualified on paper but she hadn't a clue about community medicine or interacting with people. She didn't last more than a couple of weeks.'

'Well, she left her mark,' Kate informed him, thinking of the time it had taken poor Louise to find the courage to come back for help.

'What do you mean?'

Kate told him the bare bones of what had happened, seeing the thunderous look on his face, listening to the angry tirade against Dr Myers as he slid off the desk and paced her room. 'I had no idea.'

'It's not your fault, Conor. How could you have known?'

'Poor Louise.' Swearing under his breath, he dragged the fingers of one hand through his wayward hair and she looked away, dismayed how much her own fingers itched to follow the path of his. 'Why didn't she come to me or Fred?'

Reining in her inappropriate thoughts, Kate frowned, unsure how much to tell him because she guessed Louise wouldn't want Conor to know about her crush on him. 'It's been hard for her, Conor. I think she finds it easier talking to a woman.'

'I'm glad you were here for her.' His voice husky, he closed the gap between them again. 'Thank you.'

Staring into mesmerising green eyes, she feared she was in danger of losing something of herself. 'Just doing my job,' she replied, unable to look away.

'No. It's more than that. And I appreciate it. Louise and your other patients are very lucky.'

She felt herself flushing at his compliment. 'Thank you. Um, do you know who would be likely to do the ultrasound when I refer Louise?' she asked, trying to restore order to her thoughts and banish the unwanted awareness of Conor as a man.

'Dee Miller would be your best bet,' he advised, making her nervous as he perched himself back on her desk, far too close for comfort.

'When we have an appointment confirmed I thought I would ring and have a chat to explain Louise's genuine anxiety. I hope they'll be a bit gentle with her.'

'Good idea.' His approval and understanding warmed some of the chill spots deep inside her, places she'd never expected to feel anything again. 'I'm sure they'll do all they can to put her at ease. Maybe you could persuade Louise to have an ultrasound to check for fibroids at the same time and save her the anxiety of two visits.'

Kate wasn't sure if Louise could handle more than one thing at a time. 'I'll think about it.'

'There's an excellent female gynae consultant at the county hospital. Let me know if you want me to introduce you.'

'I'll remember that, thanks.'

Kate was amazing. Conor couldn't stop looking at her, wishing he could linger there all day, talking with her. It was true he'd had reservations about her appointment—was still concerned on a personal level about her secrets and inner pain—but she was an incredible doctor, the best locum they had ever had. He was livid about Dr Myers, concerned what else the woman had done in the short time she had been with them, and he planned to review as many of the cases she had handled as possible to ensure no one else had been suffering in silence, as Louise Kerr had done. Kate was the complete opposite of Dr Myers—caring, thoughtful, dedicated. What she had done for Louise today had been important, special. He planned to do everything he could to make Kate a permanent fixture, not just at the practice but in his life…his perfect partner.

'May I cook you dinner tonight?' he asked, watching as she picked at her sandwich.

'I don't think so.'

A pout of dissatisfaction shaped his mouth. 'Why not?'

'I have things to do.'

'What things?' he pressed, unwilling to be fobbed off.

Her nervous glance flicked over him and away again. 'Private things.'

'Right.' He folded his arms, amused at her feeble excuse, noting the tinge of colour wash her cheeks. 'I'd really like to cook for you.'

'It wouldn't be a good idea, Conor,' she insisted, her voice flat and guarded.

He raised an eyebrow, teasing her. 'I'm not going to poison you.'

'I didn't mean that.'

'Kate, am I paying for someone else's sins?'

She looked shocked and wary as she glanced up in response to his softly voiced question. 'What you mean?'

'You labelled me from day one. I don't know why. But the image you have of me is wrong.' Shifting, he slid his hands under his legs, heat flooding his veins as he caught the way her gaze lingered on his thigh before she swallowed and closed her eyes. He might be as frustrated as hell but it gave him a measure of satisfaction to know Kate was not as unaffected as she pretended to be. 'You thought something was going on between me and Jenny, didn't you?' he continued, seeing her flush. 'And that wasn't the first time. So why do you always think the worst of me?'

He thought she wasn't going to answer, she was silent for so long, then she sighed and pushed the remains of her sandwich aside. 'Let's just say I knew someone who cut a swathe through the medical and clerical staff.'

'He hurt you.'

'At the time. I learned the lesson, though.'

'What lesson?' He wished she would look at him so he could gauge her expression. 'That all men are the same?'

She shook her head, one hand moving to flick a fall of hair back behind her shoulder. 'Not to get involved with colleagues.'

'Doesn't that rather depend on the circumstances and the person?' he challenged softly.

'Conor…'

As her voice trailed off, he reached out and caught her chin, tipping her face up so he could look into her eyes. Clearly her past experience was making her wary about trusting him now but he could see that this issue was not the main cause of her inner pain and the loss of professional confidence. Unfortunately they were pressed for time now and, hearing staff moving along the corridor, he reluctantly released his hold on Kate's silky-smooth skin and slid off her desk. He'd made some headway today—at least he knew why she was wary of embarking on a relationship—but there was still a long way to go if he was ever going to get beneath the surface and discover the secrets Kate kept hidden.

CHAPTER EIGHT

BEFORE dusk fell on the Saturday after Easter, Kate strolled along the sandy beach that edged the curve of the bay to where the ground rose up to a craggy headland. After a wet, grey week today had been sunny, but the April air was chilly and she drew her coat around her, sinking her hands deep into her pockets. Apart from the couple of days her father had been there, she had not yet explored this beautiful and varied landscape. Her gaze strayed out over the Solway Firth. On a clear day, she could see the Cambrian mountains on the English side to the south. Aside from a couple of people walking their dogs, the beach was deserted. She welcomed the solitude after the hectic week, although time alone with her troubled thoughts was not always a good thing. What had possessed her to reveal anything to Conor? Far from putting him off, her explanation had intrigued him further. Stopping for a moment, she breathed in the clear fresh air.

The sudden arrival of an enthusiastic and very wet dog startled her. The black-and-white cocker spaniel dropped a disreputable-looking tennis ball at her feet and grinned up at her, tongue lolling as it panted happily, stubby tail wagging twenty to the dozen.

'Hello there.' She smiled, bending to stroke the dog. 'Where did you come from?'

She glanced around to see if the owner was in sight, alarmed when she recognised Conor approaching. Oh, help. Her insides tightened at the sight of him dressed in a pair of faded jeans that lovingly hugged his legs like a second skin and a well-worn waxed jacket pulled over a fleecy jumper. He was impossibly good-looking. As he neared her, she noticed the frayed rip in one leg of his jeans, which afforded a tantalising glimpse of his thigh. Her traitorous fingers itched to touch, to explore. She turned to avoid his gaze and continued walking, unsurprised when he fell into step beside her, and she watched out of the corner of her eye as he threw the ball, the dog bounding away to retrieve it.

'Hi, Kate.'

The warm huskiness of his accented voice raised prickles on her skin. 'Hi. Have you suddenly acquired a dog?' she said, cursing her inane words.

'Sadly not. This is Toby,' he said as the dog raced back to them. Conor threw the ball once more. 'He belongs to old Dave Mackay in the village. Dave can't get out much now so he lets me borrow Toby for a walk.'

Making out that Dave was doing him the favour and not the other way round, which was typical of the Conor she was coming to know and which made him all the more dangerous to her resolve to stay away from him. They walked on for a while in silence, enjoying the tranquillity, and she indulged herself, watching Conor play with Toby. Concerned things were becoming too companionable, she decided to leave Conor to his walk with the dog and turn back before she reached the rugged headland where the rocky cliff sloped down to meet the sea.

'I'm going to head home now.' She halted, raising a hand to push her windblown hair out of her eyes.

'I'll walk back with you.'

Her heart thudded. 'You don't have to do that.'

'I know.' Conor faced her, the expression in those in-

credible green eyes far too intimate. She held her breath as
he reached out to catch a wayward strand of hair, his fingers
brushing her skin as he tucked it behind her ear. 'I want to.
Besides,' he added, fingers lingering before he turned and
whistled for the dog, 'I don't keep Toby out too long. He's
Dave's only company.'

She bit her lip to silence further protests as they retraced
their path back along the shore towards the village, which
nestled in the wooded glen at the foot of the hills.

'What are you doing tomorrow?' Conor asked, throwing
the tennis ball for Toby again.

Kate glanced at him warily. Did he never give up? 'Just
some things at home.'

'It's supposed to be a beautiful day, according to the
weather forecast. A shame to spend it all indoors.' He slipped
Toby's lead back on as they moved up off the beach. 'If you
like walking, you ought to see Glen Trool while you're here
and get up in the hills.'

'It sounds interesting. I'll do that some time,' she agreed,
keen to put distance between them.

'I'll pick you up at nine tomorrow. Dress warm and wear
walking boots if you have them.'

Shocked, she stared at him, disconcerted by the teasing
smile and the knowing look in his green eyes. 'But I—'

'See you in the morning.'

Without giving her a chance to respond, he dropped a brief
kiss on her startled lips and then strode off up a side road,
Toby trotting beside him. Bewildered, she watched his retreat-
ing figure, the fingers of one hand pressing to her mouth
where the feel of his gentle kiss lingered. Pulling herself
together, she walked the short distance to the surgery, anxious
for the sanctuary of her flat above. Conor made her feel out
of control and she didn't like it. Why was he so determined
to spend time with her? She wouldn't go tomorrow. Of course
she wouldn't. She'd make up an excuse and put him off.

Avoiding him would be much better for both of them. Feeling better about things, she made herself some hot chocolate and settled down to catch up on her medical journals. Everything would be fine. She would tell Conor she had changed her mind.

So why did she find herself sitting beside him on Sunday morning as he drove through the forest to a car park by Loch Trool? When Conor had arrived she had opened her mouth to tell him she wasn't going but her protests had been silenced by his boyish enthusiasm and her common sense had vanished—again. There had been a difficult moment when she had put on her walking boots, her gaze drawn to the dust of Africa that still lingered in the grooves and crevices from the last time she had worn them.

'What's wrong?'

'N-nothing.' Fingers shaking, she had tied the laces, pushing the memories aside, her throat tightening when she had straightened and her gaze had clashed with his, the green eyes reflecting a disturbing mix of concern, puzzlement and interest.

Conor eased her nerves by keeping off personal topics on the drive, telling her about the area they were visiting, the history of the Galloway hills, the Covenanters and Robert the Bruce, the bloodshed of centuries past hard to imagine with the tranquil beauty around them.

'What on earth have you got in here?' she complained as she helped heave his rucksack out of the boot of the car.

Green eyes shone with amusement. 'A few essentials. And a picnic lunch.'

'You said a walk, not a day trip!'

'You'll love it,' he promised. 'Everything we'll need is in there and I've left note of our route and expected return time.'

Even the weather had obeyed him. It was a warm spring day, the sky was clear and the sun shone over some of the most glorious scenery she had ever seen. Conor shouldered his pack as if it weighed nothing and gestured across the car park.

'Before we head up in the hills, come and see Bruce's Stone,' he suggested, leading the way a few hundred metres down the path and out to a small promontory where the stone stood.

'Wow,' she breathed, taking in the view across the loch.

'Lovely, isn't it?' Conor smiled and she was far too aware of his presence beside her. 'Wait until we get higher up.'

Conor breathed in the freshness of the air and tried to remember when he had last felt so contented. He didn't push the pace, aware Kate wasn't used to this, delighted to spend time with her, especially being able to share one of his favourite places. It was clear she had been going to back out that morning but he'd managed to breeze it out. There had been a peculiar moment when she had put on her boots. She had gone into a trance, just like that day at Nic and Hannah's, but the dark inner pain in her eyes when she had looked up had torn at his gut. Now she seemed to be enjoying her surroundings. After her initial fears that first day she had settled beautifully into her doctor role and everyone loved her, patients and staff alike. Outside work she held something of herself back and he knew she refused offers of social company, not just his own. She wasn't unfriendly, just private and guarded, protecting herself. Kate intrigued him more with every passing day.

'The Merrick is the highest mountain in south-west Scotland,' he told her when they stopped for a break. 'In fact, the Galloway hills are known as "The Highlands of the South".'

They walked on, pausing often to admire the views, and he pointed out things of note, finding Kate an avid listener. She showed a keen interest in everything, asking questions as they passed from the glen to the uplands, the glacial landscape becoming more remote, changing to moorland and mountains. He was surprised to discover that Kate wasn't as physically fit as he'd anticipated, so he kept things gentle and watched her closely to ensure she was comfortable. Again he remembered how pale and stressed she had been when she had first arrived in Glentown. She had more colour now and she had put on some weight, which certainly suited her, he decided, casting an appreciative glance over her delicious curves. He wondered again if she had been unwell. More than once he noticed her left hand stray to her side and he paused as they passed Loch Neldricken to give her another chance to rest before they headed on along the slope of Ewe Rig, enjoying the solitude, and then began the harder climb towards Redstone Rig.

Finding it hard to catch her breath on the steepest parts, Kate was grateful that Conor kept the pace gentle, although she envied the effortless way he moved up the trail ahead of her. She hadn't realised how much the events of recent months had taken out of her but now she felt her legs would seize any moment. She had healed physically but had not done much exercise in the last weeks and now she was feeling it. Maybe this had been a touch ambitious. But saying so would require an explanation and that she couldn't give, so she kept going. Unconsciously her hand clasped her left side below her ribs where an ache twinged.

'Something wrong, Kate?'

Alarmed that Conor had seen her action, she removed her hand. 'Nothing,' she lied, but she could tell he didn't believe her and was both curious and concerned. 'Just a stitch,' she fabricated, hoping to divert his attention and head off any further questions.

'A bit out of practice?' he teased, going along with her subterfuge as he shrugged off his rucksack and waited for her to join him. 'We'll have to make sure you get more physical activity while you're here.'

She could feel a flush colour her already heated cheeks at

the wicked glint in his eyes. She could just imagine the kind of physical activity he had in mind and no way was that going to happen! 'I'm fine.' At least she had diverted him from anything else that might be wrong.

'Well, what do you think?'

'About what?' She propped herself against the nearest available outcrop for support.

'Him,' Conor elaborated, pointing towards a rock formation which, in profile, created the perfect likeness of a wizened, aged face. 'The Grey Man.'

Momentarily blind to the breathtaking scenery all around her, Kate stared. 'You brought me all the way up here to see a rock?'

'It's not just a rock.' He laughed, disgustingly unflustered. 'Isn't it fabulous?'

It was impressive, she had to concede, her equilibrium returning after a short rest. Her father would love it, too. Conor was in his element here. He not only knew so much about the landscape and history but she realised how much of his rare free time he spent walking in the hills and forests or along the coastal paths, either alone or with his friends and fellow GPs Kyle and Nic. Did that mean his other ladies came here, too? Not that she was one of them, she added with a frown. But if he worked so hard, walked so much and played other sports, how did he have time for all his liaisons? He'd been to visit Lizzie in hospital, done other favours for people, but she couldn't remember hearing of Conor actually dating anyone in the whole time she had been there. So was she wrong about him? If she was, it made him more dangerous and her more vulnerable.

Conor found a sheltered spot and they settled down to their picnic lunch, enjoying the sunshine and the incredible views. Ribbons of gossamer cloud streamed around the highest peaks, some of which still had a coating of snow, looking as if some giant celestial hand had dusted them with icing sugar. They chatted about the scenery, the remote tranquillity inspiring awe and reverence, and then talk turned to work and Conor mentioned Fred.

'He's been fabulous to work with.' Conor leaned back, resting on his elbows. 'But he has been slowing down these last months and I worry about him. I know the day will come, probably quite soon, when he'll decide to go part time or give up completely. Not that I begrudge him his retirement but I'll miss him.'

'I was very sorry to hear about his wife.'

'Yeah. He's never picked up from losing Annette,' Conor confided, his voice wistful and sad. 'It was a bad time.'

'What will you do when Fred retires? Practice-wise, I mean.'

He glanced at her, his eyes hooded. 'I'm hoping my perfect partner will never want to leave.'

Kate looked away, unnerved by the edge to his voice, unwilling to acknowledge how much this place and these people had come to mean to her in just six weeks, how hard it was going to be for her to walk away when her contract ended. Her father had hinted she could stay on if she wanted to. Maybe she could have, if things had been different… But they weren't, so there was no point dwelling in fantasy land.

'I'm sure you'll find someone suitable when the time comes.'

She drew her knees up and wrapped her arms around them, gazing unseeing at the hills, not wanting to think about who would come after her to fill her shoes on a permanent basis and find their niche in this wonderful community…and be Conor's partner. Unsettled by her thoughts, far too conscious of him close beside her, she began packing away the things then scrabbled to her feet.

Taking a different route, they began the walk back down in silence, a growing tension fizzing between them. When she skidded on some loose shale, Conor was there to catch her, his arm strong and secure around her waist as he held her far too close for several breath-sapping moments before she managed to extract herself and put some distance between them.

'Thanks,' she mumbled, unable to look at him.

'No problem.'

His own voice was rough, letting her know he was affected and aware. This was ridiculous. She swallowed, sucking in a few deep breaths, trying to regain some control as they continued the descent, surprised when Conor took her hand to help her over the rocky path down the Buchan Burn. He failed to release her, his fingers linking with hers as they paused to look at the waterfall. Her traitorous body reacted to his touch, her pulse racing, her flesh tingling, her hormones rampaging out of control.

She was relieved when they reached the car park. The walk had been wonderful, the views amazing, and she wouldn't have missed seeing any of this for the world. The problem was her awareness of Conor, her dwindling willpower to keep him at bay. Thankful for some respite, she leaned against the car and waited while he stowed his pack in the boot, expecting him to continue round to the driver's side to unlock the doors. So when he walked towards her, moving in close, her heart began beating a wild tattoo in her chest.

He was way too close. Kate swallowed, nerves jangling inside her. He put his hands on the car roof either side of her head, holding her captive. She couldn't breathe. Mesmerising green eyes were dark and intent. Whatever fragments of self-control she had left were shot to pieces. If he touched her now she was going to explode. Scared how vulnerable she was to him, her hands rose to his chest in a futile effort to maintain some distance between them.

'Conor—'

'I enjoyed myself today.'

'Um, yes, it was good. Walking,' she managed, her voice far too husky and unsteady.

His sultry gaze dropped to her mouth as she moistened dry lips. 'I meant being with you.'

'I don't think—'

'Good,' he interrupted, brushing the pad of his thumb across her mouth to silence her. 'Don't think, Kate. Just feel.'

The first touch of his mouth on hers threatened to make her breathless all over again. His initial kiss was hesitant, as if assessing her reaction, his lips warm and coaxing as he encouraged a response. Not that he needed to. Much to her despair, her body was betraying her brain. No matter how much she denied this, her mouth was taking on a will of its own as her lips parted in shameless invitation, seeking more, demanding more.

She heard Conor's soft moan as he gave her what she craved. One arm slid round her waist and drew her closer against him, while his other hand sank into her hair, cupping the back of her neck as he changed the angle, deepening the kiss, moving from teasing gentleness to heated demand. It wasn't fair. He was far, far too good at this.

She whimpered, her whole body on fire as Conor sucked erotically on her lower lip before his tongue slid into her mouth, placing teasing strokes on hers, encouraging it to join in a sensual dance. The passion erupted between them, flaring out of control. It wasn't enough. She wanted more, wanted everything, needed to climb right inside his skin.

Forgetting where they were, her hands burrowed under his jacket, her fingers pulling restlessly at the hem of his jumper and the shirt beneath, impatient to feel the touch of his skin, finding his back warm and supple, the muscles flexing. His earthy scent made her light-headed, his taste made her feel drunk. It had been a while since she had been with a man, been held and kissed. Not that she'd ever been kissed like *this* before. It was all heat and fire and sensual seduction. Slow, deep, thorough, unbelievably sexual as he made love to her with his mouth. And she wanted more. Much more.

Conor shifted even closer, the length of his athletic body pressing along hers, leaving her in no doubt about the extent of his arousal. But he still wasn't close enough. She moved more firmly against him, desperate to ease the terrible burning ache that raged inside her, moaning in relief as he slid one leg between hers. Too needy to care what she was doing, she wantonly rubbed herself on his thigh, matching the suggestive rhythm of his movements. The hand at her waist slid down to cup her rear, pulling her tighter. He tilted his chest to one side and she gasped into his mouth as his other hand burrowed under her jacket to shape the fullness of her breast, her hardened nipple urgently seeking his palm, a fiery ache of sensation short-circuiting to her womb.

She wanted to tell him there were too many clothes between them but no way on earth could she break this earth-shatteringly sensual kiss. Their mouths fitted like two halves of a whole, lips clinging, caressing, taking and giving every-thing, tongues tasting, teasing, joining in an impassioned ex-ploration. But the urge to satisfy the burning need was becoming too much to bear. Her fingers moved more insis-tently on his back as she lost herself in the magic of getting physical with Conor Anderson, sharing what was the most in-tensely erotic and arousing experience of her life. Just when she was unable to help herself squirming more blatantly against him, her hands working round to the fastening of his jeans, Conor was pulling away.

'No!' Unaware of what she was doing, she protested, trying to hold onto him. 'Please.'

His hands cupped her face and she struggled to open her eyes, staring dazedly into the heated green depths of his, her heart racing, each ragged breath searing her lungs. He held her away from him, fighting for control. Part of her wanted to weep because he had stopped and she needed him so badly, while another part of her was ashamed that she had so lost control that she would have let him—made him—take her here in a public car park, and damn the consequences.

* * *

Conor wanted to cry with frustration. Dazed, disbelieving, he held onto Kate and fought to regain his senses, cursing fate for doing this to them.

'I'm sorry, we have to stop.'

'Conor?'

'We're needed. Listen.'

His shaky, breathless words seemed to permeate Kate's confusion as she turned her head towards the source of the insistent background noise before glazed brown eyes struggled to focus on his face. 'What?'

'Someone's in trouble.'

The last thing in the world he wanted was to let her go. He wasn't even sure he could move because his knees were so shaky and he was so painfully aroused, all his senses in a spin after what had to be the most mind-numbing kiss he'd ever shared in his life.

What the hell had happened to them? It was crazy. One moment he'd brushed her lips with his, the next it had been as if the whole universe had imploded, spinning him away in a vortex of heat and pleasure, and he'd been lost in her sweetness, the clamouring rush of sexual demand. Dear heaven.

He looked down at her flushed face and the dusky-rose lips still trembling and swollen, groaning aloud as he forced himself to move, to set her away from him before he lost it again, still shocked that he'd been so carried away that he'd forgotten where they were. As much as he needed her, he certainly didn't want their first time together to be some rushed and thoughtless moment against his car in a public place. No way. He wanted to take his time and savour every inch of her body, every second of loving her.

Dragging a shaky hand through his tousled hair, he stumbled away from her, every atom of him screaming to finish what they had started, but he could see the woman who had been calling for help as she emerged from the path into the car park. In her sixties, dishevelled, tears streaming down her face, she hurried towards them.

'Please, someone, help!'

'What's happened?' Conor called.

'My husband, Angus,' the woman sobbed. 'It's his heart.'

Taking the woman by the arm, he steered her to the car, somehow managing to organise his thoughts as he used his mobile to call for emergency assistance, asking for the local park ranger as well as the nearest paramedics or the air ambulance, whichever would be quicker to reach this remote spot. He was thankful to note that Kate had similarly snapped into professional mode, at least on the outside. Inside he imagined she was as wired as he was. His whole body throbbed with unfulfilled want, her fragrance and her taste filling his senses. As Kate took his keys and went to the boot of the car, he pushed his own needs aside and focused on the distressed woman, trying to extract a medical history.

'What's your name?'

'R-Rose,' the woman cried.

'OK, Rose. We're both doctors. We'll do all we can to help him. Does Angus have a history of heart trouble?'

The woman nodded, her whole body trembling as she leaned against the car. 'Yes. For years. He's already had one triple bypass,' she explained, giving details of his medications.

'Does he have a pacemaker fitted?' The woman shook her head and he was sympathetic to her distress while cursing the wasted time. 'Whereabouts is Angus, Rose?'

'Down the path by Bruce's Stone.'

He nodded as Kate took the emergency bag and automated external defibrillator from the secure compartment in the boot of his car before running on ahead. 'I'll bring the oxygen and be right behind you,' he told her, turning back to Rose. 'I know this is hard but I need you to keep calm. Please, wait here and direct the park ranger or paramedics to us. Can you do that?'

'Yes. B-but—'

'Rose, we've no time to waste if we're to help Angus.'

Leaving the poor woman at the car, he grabbed the oxygen from the boot and took off after Kate. When he caught up with her, she was kneeling by the man who was lying on the path. She already had his shirt open and the adhesive electrode pads that recorded ECG and delivered the shock attached to the chest.

'How is he?'

'Unresponsive. No pulse and he's not breathing.' She checked the trace on the machine while administering chest compressions. 'Conor, he's in VF.'

While the machine charged, ready to deliver a shock, Conor tilted the man's head back and raised his chin, working swiftly to clear the airway and insert an endotracheal tube. 'Bilateral breath sounds,' he confirmed once the oxygen was attached and he monitored the adequate chest rises.

'I'll get a line in if you can take over here.'

He prepared to continue uninterrupted chest compressions, calling 'Clear' as the machine readied for the first shock and he watched Kate attend to the oxygen before pressing the button. The machine recharged and a series of three shocks was delivered without altering the VF rhythm. Resuming the oxygen supply, he returned to chest compressions as Kate struggled to find a vein, muttering darkly as her first two attempts failed. 'Cannula in. 1milligram of adrenalin?'

'Yes. Flush with 20 to 30 mils of saline.'

'OK.'

There were no anti-arrythmic drugs in the bag so they continued with the cycle of shocks, compressions and flush of adrenalin, the trace on the machine showing the irregular wave form of VF. Once they appeared to have Angus back, the AED trace confirming a change in rhythm, a carotid pulse vaguely discernible, but within minutes the machine alerted them to a return of VF and they renewed the sequence of adrenalin, shock and compressions.

'Hello?' a voice called, and Conor glanced up, seeing one of the park rangers he knew running down the path.

'Here, Gavin.'

'I didn't know it was you, Conor. That's a blessing. Air ambulance ETA is five minutes. They were nearby after a patient transfer. The closest landing site with road access is three miles away,' the ranger explained with a grimace. 'We've arranged to drive them up straight away and will transport your patient down when you're set to go.'

Conor nodded. 'Thanks, Gavin. Is someone taking care of the wife, Rose?'

'It's being done.'

Gavin went to organise things but it seemed for ever before two paramedics arrived, a couple of volunteers waiting nearby to help with the stretcher. 'What have we got, Doc?'

Conor filled them in on Angus's known history, what they had done, the drugs administered and the time they had been attempting resuscitation. 'Do you have amiodarone?'

'I do. Standard 300 milligrams IV bolus diluted in 20 mils of 5 per cent dextrose?'

'Thanks.'

'Lucky you happened to be here,' the first paramedic commented, and Conor glanced at Kate, seeing her flush, remembering all too clearly what they had been doing before they had been interrupted by the emergency.

They worked as a team to do all they could for Angus, but Conor feared the outcome was not hopeful, despite all their efforts. When the AED trace confirmed Angus had the return of an output, Conor began clearing his things. 'Let's get going before we lose him again.'

As post-resuscitation care continued, willing hands helped carry the stretcher to the car park and slid it into a park vehicle for the journey to the air ambulance.

'We have room if one of you wants to come with us,' a paramedic suggested.

'I'll go,' Kate offered. 'Then you can bring Rose in the car.'

Not wanting to waste time, Conor nodded, following the convoy of park vehicles to the site where the yellow helicopter awaited them. Asking a distressed Rose to wait for him, Conor ran to help the others load Angus on board, checking his precarious condition and ensuring Kate was OK.

'You sure you're all right to do this?' he said.

'I'll be fine.'

'I'll drive his wife down and meet you there.'

He hated sending Kate off without him but in the circumstances there was no time to waste. Every second counted for Angus. Conor squeezed Kate's hand for a second before he was forced to stand back as she climbed inside. All he could see was Kate's face at the window as, moments later, the aircraft lifted into the sky and headed south-east. Filled with an urgency to go to her, he hurried back to the car, doing his best to comfort Rose as they started the longer road journey to town.

CHAPTER NINE

ANOTHER day was over but even with Fred back full time, work was still hectic. Louise Kerr had been for another follow-up consultation, still nervous but happy to report some improvement in her various symptoms. The urine sample had shown no signs of diabetes and Kate hoped she could persuade the young woman to go for the ultrasound when the appointment came through from the hospital. It was going to be a long haul but it was rewarding being able to help someone in need. She was sad she wouldn't be there long term to see Louise through her whole journey.

Frowning, she raised her arms above her head, closing her eyes as she stretched her body, trying to tease out some of the knots that tightened her muscles—muscles that hadn't fully recovered from the hours hiking in the hills with Conor three days ago. No. She didn't want to remember Sunday for all sorts of reasons.

'Would you like me to give you a massage?'

The teasing suggestion had her eyes snapping open, warmth heating her cheeks as Conor appeared at her consulting-room doorway, two steaming mugs held in his hands.

'No, thanks,' she declined, suppressing a shiver at the thought of feeling Conor's touch on her body again.

'You only have to ask if you change your mind.'

Kate knew he was talking about much more than the massage and her stomach tightened, warmth prickling through her. Wary, she watched as he crossed the room, the scent of hot chocolate teasing her and making her mouth water almost as much as the memory of their erotic kiss.

'Thanks,' she murmured as he set a mug down for her, perturbed at their shared passion for hot chocolate.

Shared passions with Conor was a taboo subject. Especially after Sunday's lapse in self-control. She could feel his gaze on her as he sat down, cupping his own mug in his hands, and she prayed he wasn't going to raise the thorny subject of the kiss again. He was frustrated with her because she had panicked at what could have happened, at her brazen behaviour, and she had insisted she didn't want to talk about it—or repeat it. Which was a lie, because her body wanted to, whatever her head tried to tell it. Everything was so complicated in her life and she felt so edgy, but she was grateful that, although Conor didn't understand, he'd respected her wishes. So far. How long either of them could keep up the pretence she was too nervous to consider.

'I had a chat with Rose today,' he said after a few tense moments of silence, and a wave of sadness hit her, her own concerns set aside as she glanced up and saw the understanding in Conor's green eyes.

'How is she coping?'

'As well as can be expected. She's going home to Manchester tomorrow. Her son has flown home from his business trip to Germany and is coming up to fetch her.' He paused a moment, sipping his drink. 'You were out on house calls when she rang but she asked me to thank you for all you did.'

Kate frowned. 'Whatever that was.'

Angus had never regained consciousness. His condition had remained unstable on the short helicopter journey and he had crashed again at the hospital, the efforts of the emergency team failing to resuscitate him. The latest massive event had been too much for Angus's heart to bear and by the time Conor had arrived at A and E with Rose, Angus had died.

'We did all we could, Kate,' Conor reassured her, the warm huskiness of his voice sending a customary tingle down her spine. 'With his past medical history and the state in which we found him, Angus's chances of survival were poor from the outset.'

'I know.'

The incident with Angus had made her think of other lives she might have saved had her skills and her nerve been adequate, but she couldn't explain that to Conor, had never talked about it, not even with her father or the professor. She couldn't talk about it. Couldn't face it herself. Closing her eyes to evade Conor's observation, she leaned back and tasted her drink, her thoughts returning to Sunday. It had been late by the time they'd arrived back in Glentown and she had insisted Conor drop her at the flat, knowing he had been confused and concerned by the distance she had placed between them. But she hadn't been able to face him, too vulnerable to put herself in the danger zone again and be tempted to forget everything in his arms. It would be good but reality would return afterwards. Somehow, if she wanted to regain her career and her life, she had to face all the issues that Conor had so scarily and correctly identified were eating her up inside.

Her eyes opened, finding him watching her, and a ripple of unease went through her. She wasn't sure she had the courage to confront those demons, scared that if she let go she would never put the pieces back together again.

Conor watched the play of emotions cross Kate's face, having a good idea where her thoughts were travelling. She had panicked after Sunday's explosive kiss, refusing to talk about it, her assertion that it was unimportant, a momentary lapse, making him annoyed and frustrated. He had reluctantly backed off, concerned he would push her further away if he pressured her because instinct told him there were other issues complicating things. But now Sunday had become yet another no-go area. If Kate thought she could lie to herself that the kiss hadn't meant anything, so be it, but no way was he going to accept that. What they shared was special and now he'd had a taste of paradise, he was going to fight to keep it. If that meant changing tactics in an attempt to draw her out of her comfort zone until she faced up to whatever she was burying, then he would do it. And to hell with playing fair. This was too important…for both of them.

Sensing her unease, Conor sipped his chocolate, his gaze watchful as he planned the next stage of his campaign. 'I also heard from Nic and Hannah today,' he told her, seeing interest vie with the wariness in her soulful brown eyes.

'Are they OK?'

'Fine. They're coming over at the weekend with the kittens.' He smiled at the flash of excitement she couldn't hide and leaned forward to set his empty mug on the desk. 'They said to say hello and that they are looking forward to seeing you.'

Wariness came to the fore again. 'Oh, but—'

'I was hoping you'd visit the pet shop with me. I'd be grateful for your help deciding what the kittens will need,' he interrupted, tempting her before she could formulate an excuse.

'Well…' She trailed off, even white teeth nibbling her lower lip and making his gut—and other parts of him—tighten with desire. 'When did you have in mind?'

Keeping things light and trying not to show his elation that she hadn't flat out refused, he gave a casual shrug. 'I thought we could go to Rigtownbrae on Saturday after surgery finishes at lunchtime.'

'I guess that would be OK.'

'Great. Thanks, Kate.' Hiding his relief at her agreement, he rose to his feet, forcing himself to leave it there and not push yet about joining Nic and Hannah at his house for a meal. He had to take a step at a time if he hoped to regain lost ground and reach a point where she trusted him enough to let go and confide in him.

Noting the surprise and confusion on her face as he made to leave, he gave her a friendly smile and headed for the door. 'I'll look forward to Saturday.'

'We've bought an awful lot,' Kate said as she helped Conor unload their purchases of food, bowls, litter trays, beds, toys and other accessories when they returned to Glentown-on-Firth late on Saturday afternoon.

'I'm glad you were there to help me. Thank you.'

She frowned as he smiled and continued to take things out of the car. His behaviour over the last few days had confused her. She had expected him to pressure her but he'd been friendly and warm without overstepping her boundaries. It should have pleased her but she felt even more unsettled and fidgety. Did it mean he'd lost interest? If so, that was a good thing. Wasn't it? Her frown deepened. If only she could get the feel of him, the taste of him, the memory of that sexy kiss out of her mind. But she couldn't. And she was even more confused. She wasn't sure it was a good idea to spend time with him but the thought of the kittens was irresistible.

They had been late leaving as Sheena McIntosh had brought little Callie to the surgery, the child who had made a fuss having her arm stitched. With her teddy bear, still sporting Conor's stitches, clutched in one hand, she had handed over a sheet of paper covered in abstract blotches of bright colours.

'I drawed this for you,' she announced proudly.

Smiling, Conor dropped to his knees in front of her. 'Thank you, sweetie. I'll put it in my kitchen.'

Kate's heart had turned, watching him with Callie, devoting his attention and sweeping her into his arms for a cuddle. He'd make such a wonderful father—if only he wasn't so against commitment. She looked at him now, adding Callie's messy picture to the pile of things to be taken inside, knowing many other people would have thrown it away when the child had gone. Turning away in confusion, she concentrated instead on her first sight of his house.

Situated on rising ground at the edge of the village and reached by a short, secluded drive, the house was set back from the road and out of sight of its neighbours. Built of granite, partly painted white, it was long and low, one half single-storey with a flat roof and the other half double-storey under a pitched slate roof with two squat chimneys. From the sweep of the gravel drive she could see part of the huge garden, which was sheltered by trees and shrubs and afforded views over the Firth to the south and to the woods and hills to the north. It was stunning and she loved it the moment she set eyes on it.

'Come along in,' Conor invited her, hoisting several bags into his arms and leading the way.

Picking up a few packages, she followed him and found herself in a big, homely kitchen with a slate floor, rustic table and filled with welcoming warmth from a Rayburn. The room had pale wood units, slate worktops and was decorated in creams, pastel yellows and pastel blues. Sunshine flooded in through a large window and a pair of glass doors at one end that looked out towards the coast. Kate had no idea what she had expected of the place Conor lived, but it wasn't this. She felt at home, at peace. Which was scary. Sensing him watching her, she turned away and set down the bags, nervous now she was alone with him on his own territory. He collected the last of the things, returning to the kitchen to unpack everything, glancing at her with a sheepish smile.

'It does look rather a lot, doesn't it?'

'They're going to be two very spoiled kittens.'

Warm green eyes looked at her. 'I like spoiling those special to me.'

Her pulse rate rose and a tingle of awareness shivered through her. For a moment she didn't think she could breathe, then Conor moved away, releasing her from his spell, and she sucked air into her parched lungs. Feeling shaky, she watched as he fixed Callie's artwork to the big fridge with a couple of magnets, the painting joining an assorted collection of photos, cards and funny quotations. Next he took out a couple of glasses and then opened a bottle of red wine, letting it stand for a few moments while he returned to the fridge, taking out an enormous dish topped with mashed potatoes which he put into one of the Rayburn's ovens.

'Hannah will skin me alive if her fish pie isn't ready!' He smiled, returning to pour the wine. 'She and Nic will be here soon.'

'I was going to go home. I thought—' Her words snapped off and she wondered how she was to extract herself from this situation.

'That would be a shame—they'd be upset not to see you.'

She bit her lip, suspicious that Conor had tricked her into this. 'I didn't realise they were bringing the kittens today.'

'That's why I was in a rush to get the things.' His expression looked innocent as he handed her a glass. 'Here you go. Try this.'

'Thanks.'

Conor turned away, moving back to the fridge and taking out salad ingredients. 'I arranged for them to go and see Charlie—he's called the puppy Ben, by the way. Nic and Hannah are coming here afterwards. Feel free to wander around and make yourself at home.'

Kate hovered for a moment, torn between wanting to escape and genuine pleasure at the thought of seeing Hannah and Nic again. Not to mention the kittens. She took a fortifying sip of wine, watching from beneath her lashes as Conor prepared the food, impressed with his easy dexterity. Curious to see more of the house and needing space from the intensity of being close to him, she wandered out of the kitchen that was at the single-storey end of the house. A light passage-way led to a small formal dining room and a flight of stairs led up from the hall to the upper storey. She bypassed the stairs, finding a small cloakroom and then a study, where Conor clearly spent a fair amount of time. A similar-sized room came next and was packed with shelves of books. She browsed a while, finding a mix of local history, environment, biographies, sport and some novels. Moving on, the last re-maining room was the living room. It was beautiful. In the old part of the house, the beamed ceilings were lower but the room was light, large windows and French doors looking out over the wonderful garden and the views to the south and south-west. The plain walls, painted a pale terracotta, made the atmosphere even more cosy and warm. At the other end was an inviting inglenook fireplace and she could imagine curling up on one of the sofas and snuggling up in front of that fire on a freezing winter night. Alarmed at the direction of her thoughts, she spun away and crossed to gaze out at the garden.

She sensed rather than heard Conor's approach, glancing over her shoulder as he came into the room with an armful of logs.

'OK, sweetheart?'

'Fine,' she murmured, watching as he knelt down by the fire and swiftly coaxed it to life. 'Your house is lovely.'

'Thank you. I fell in love with it as soon as I saw it and I'm really happy here. Did you see upstairs?'

'No.' Upstairs meant bedrooms and that was far too dan-gerous and tempting.

'The views from the terrace are wonderful.'

It wasn't the views she was worried about! She was saved from further difficulties by the sound of a car arriving outside, and Conor rose to his feet, setting a guard in front of the fire.

'Let's go and see our kittens!'

Kate wanted to point out that they were nothing to do with

her, but he had already set off along the passageway. She followed more slowly, feeling out of place, but Hannah and Nic greeted her with enthusiasm and she was soon drawn into their circle, her nerves dissipating.

'I can't believe how much they've grown in such a short time!' she exclaimed as Nic set down the travel basket and Hannah handed one frisky grey kitten to Conor and one to her.

She cradled it in her arms, realising it was the one with the little white mark on its front. They seemed not to have been bothered by their journey, settling down for a cuddle, trying to outdo each other with the loudness of their purring.

'You're certainly well prepared! You have a whole pet shop in here.' Hannah laughed, looking around the kitchen. 'What are you going to call them, Conor?'

'I've chosen Smoky for this little girl,' he answered with a smile, looking like a proud father as he sat at the rustic table, the kitten cuddled against his chest, and Kate felt her heart clench as his green gaze met hers. 'Kate picked the other name.'

She flushed as Nic and Hannah looked at her with interested speculation, concerned they may get the wrong idea about her and Conor. 'I suggested Willow,' she replied, looking down at the contented kitten.

'Willow is a lovely name,' Nic said, his Italian accent warm and attractive.

'It suits her,' Hannah agreed with a smile. 'And Ben suits our little dog. He's looking amazing, Conor. It was so lovely to see him again, happy and settled in his new home. Charlie was full of Ben's progress and antics!'

'The change in Charlie is amazing. Thanks to Kate. The idea was inspired,' Conor added, his approval making Kate's cheeks warm and setting her pulse skittering again.

They chatted about Ben and the animals until it was time to eat. With the kittens settled in their new beds and curled up asleep after their adventurous day, Conor served up the salad and some fresh granary bread, then took the steaming, mouth-watering pie from the oven. The aroma was enough to set Kate's taste buds zinging and she wasn't the only one as Hannah took her place at the table with enthusiasm.

'Ooh, you don't know how I've been looking forward to this!' she sighed, as Conor set the dish on the table.

Laughing, Nic poured the wine before taking a seat beside his wife. 'The way she raves about your food, my friend, makes me feel inadequate,' he teased, his brown eyes full of mischief.

'If I wasn't already stuck with you, I'd marry Conor just for his cooking!' Hannah giggled at the possessive look on her husband's face. 'Don't be silly, Nic, I'm only teasing. Conor wouldn't have me anyway!'

Kate was disconcerted when Hannah smiled at her, a knowing look in her eyes. Was the other woman alluding to the fact that Conor was shy of marriage and families? She felt his gaze on her but didn't look up, concentrating on her meal as Hannah tucked into the food with appreciative sighs of enjoyment. Kate took her first mouthful of Conor's fish pie and thought she had gone to heaven. Oh, my! She closed her eyes, savouring the subtle but delectable flavours that melted on her tongue. Realising the room had gone quiet, she opened her eyes, flushing as she discovered the others watching her with amusement.

'Well?' Hannah demanded with a grin.

Kate flicked a brief glance towards Conor. 'It's lovely.'

Thankful when the conversation moved on and she was no longer the centre of attention, Kate concentrated on enjoying her food, lingering over every forkful. She didn't remember ever having tasted anything so delicious. Except for Conor himself. Heat flooded through her and she couldn't stop herself looking at him, seeing desire flare in the depths of his green eyes as his gaze met hers. She feared he knew just what she was thinking about.

Feeling edgy, Kate was glad when the evening came to an

end, fretting about whether Conor would try to delay her, surprised when he suggested Nic and Hannah drop her at the surgery on their way through the village. As the others lingered in the living room, Kate went to the kitchen to collect her things and say goodbye to the kittens. It was a wrench, leaving them, and she wished she could take them home, envying Conor their company. As she was about to leave the kitchen to rejoin the others, she heard their voices approaching.

'Kate?'

She straightened at Conor's call, casting a final glance at the sleeping kittens. 'I'm coming.'

Rejoining them in the hallway, she was grateful that Hannah and Nic bustled her out to the car without further delay, although Conor's apparent disinterest contrarily played on her mind.

Hannah turned to smile at her as Nic drove down the drive to the lane. 'Tell me you are going to come to the fundraising dinner and keep me company.'

'I don't think so.'

'Please. It wouldn't be the same without you, would it, Nic?' Hannah demanded.

She saw Nic shake his head in the dimness of the car. 'It would make us very happy to have you join us, Kate.'

'What exactly is this dinner?' she queried, not wanting to commit herself.

'Hasn't Conor told you?' Hannah protested, tutting in frustration. 'It's a charity event we have twice a year for all the local services: health professionals from hospitals and general practices; the fire service; mountain rescue; RNLI; police. Members of the public can buy tickets, too, and we raise money for necessary equipment for the hospital or the air ambulance, that kind of thing.'

'I didn't bring anything to wear to something like that,' Kate prevaricated, hoping that would be an end to it, but she had counted without Hannah's determination.

'That's no problem,' the other woman said dismissively. 'It's not formal ballgowns or anything. I know the perfect place—I'll email you the details. Aileen will tell you more about it.'

Kate was thankful when the car drew up at the surgery. 'I'll see. Thanks for the lift. It was good seeing you both again.'

'You too, Kate,' Hannah replied, warmth in her voice.

Kate opened the door, surprised when Nic climbed out as well. 'I'll walk you down, *cara*.'

'Thanks.'

At her door she searched her bag for her key before smiling at him. 'Goodnight.'

In the security light, Nic's dark eyes were kind and understanding. 'Take care, Kate. We'll hope to see you soon. Don't forget you have friends here.'

She watched him walk into the darkness, his parting words ringing in her ears. Her mind buzzing with myriad thoughts, she went inside, locked up and prepared for bed.

True to her promise, Kate found an email from Hannah in her inbox on Monday morning, giving the details of somewhere she could get a suitable outfit. Kate still wasn't sure whether to go. There were also emails from James and a couple of friends, but with a busy surgery ahead she left those for that evening when she would have more time. The final email was from Conor. She felt nervous when she opened it, wondering why he was contacting her that way, but a smile curved her mouth when she discovered he had taken digital photos of the kittens and had sent her some. After emailing a brief note of thanks, she changed her desktop screensaver to an image of Smoky and Willow then buzzed her first patient through.

As she had predicted, her morning was hectic. After her consultations she went out on home visits and it was lunchtime when she arrived back at the surgery. It was quiet when she walked in so she left her tray of notes for Jenny or Aileen to file and some correspondence she needed Barbara Allcott, their medical secretary, to prepare, then walked down the corridor towards her room. As she passed Conor's door, he glanced up and beckoned her in.

'Hi,' he greeted. 'Do you have a minute?'

'Sure,' she agreed, feeling wary as she sat down.

'I gather you've been out to see feisty Mrs Lucas at the residential home this morning?'

Kate nodded, frowning. 'Is there a problem?'

'No, of course not!' Conor looked at her in surprise. 'I wanted your impressions of the place. It's not been open long.'

'I've been there a couple of times now and I've found it excellent.'

His eyes crinkled at the corners as he smiled, leaning back in his chair and linking his hands behind his head. 'Don't look so worried. I've had an idea.'

'What about?' she queried, trying to relax and not notice the way the fabric of his T-shirt pulled across the muscles of his chest.

'Lizzie Dalglish.' Conor sat forward, taking out a set of notes. 'You know we were talking about the problems of her living with Yvonne and Billy, plus the issue of the stairs?'

'I remember. How is she coping since leaving hospital?'

'That's just it. She's been staying at the residential place to convalesce. I saw her yesterday afternoon and she was in better spirits, being back in the village with her friends able to visit her and update her on the local gossip!'

Smiling, Kate nodded. 'I can imagine. I wish I'd known she was there, I'd have stopped by. What's the problem?'

'Yvonne is talking about taking her home and either making alterations to the house or moving to a bungalow.'

'And Lizzie doesn't want to go,' Kate supplied.

Conor's smile was appreciative. 'We're clearly on the same wavelength. Lizzie is enjoying being in the hub of things—she has a unit of her own on the ground floor and is able to have some independence but with help on hand twenty-four hours a day. It's an ideal solution for her—but she's worried how Yvonne will react.' A pout of consideration shaped his mouth and drew her attention to his lips, bringing the memory of their feel and taste.

'Um, well…' She cleared her throat, forcing herself to look away. 'Have you spoken to Yvonne?'

'She and Billy have felt the burden of Lizzie's care this past year but she's adamant Lizzie should be with them,' he explained.

'Probably neither party wants to hurt the other's feelings,' Kate mused. 'Would they be all right financially if Lizzie stayed on permanently at the home? It's an impressive place.'

Conor nodded, twisting a pen through his fingers. 'I gather Lizzie has the money from the sale of her home. I'll have another chat with Yvonne this week and try to get her and Lizzie talking honestly to each other about their real feelings. Sometimes you can get so close to things you can't see the solution.'

'Right.' She rose to her feet, unsettled by the underlying edge in his voice, scared he might be alluding to her own unwillingness to confide in him. Despite being eager to escape, she lingered a moment, unable to help herself. 'Thanks for the photos. How are the kittens?'

'It's been an exhausting round of playing, eating and sleeping so far!'

'They must be a handful,' she agreed, hearing her own wistfulness.

Green eyes turned warm. 'Any time you want to come and play with them you're more than welcome.'

'Thanks.' It was tempting. But so was Conor and being at his house wasn't sensible. 'I'd best get on.'

'Hannah emailed this morning. She says you're coming to the dinner.'

His words stopped her before she reached the door. 'She asked me, but I haven't decided.'

'I hope you'll say yes, Kate.'

The sultry green gaze and husky voice made her hot right through. Temptation was becoming harder and harder to resist.

CHAPTER TEN

DEAR God!

Conor felt his whole body going into meltdown as he looked at Kate. Having managed, with Hannah's help, to cajole her into attending the fundraising dinner, he'd forced himself into a dreaded suit for the occasion, anticipation bringing him to the flat several minutes early.

'I won't be long, I'm not quite ready,' she said, and he was thankful she was unaware of his predicament, his raging desire mixed with stunned shock.

He tried to draw air into starved lungs, his gaze following her, devouring her. From the first day he had admired her natural beauty but never more so than now, the bare minimum of make-up needed to enhance brown eyes he wanted to drown in and dusky-rose lips he couldn't wait to taste again. Her dark brown hair was loose, just the way he loved it, falling in a glossy curtain to frame her face and brush her bare shoulders, a wispy fringe feathering her brow. His fingers itched to bury themselves in the silken thickness. As for her outfit… Conor swallowed the restriction in his throat. How those two minute little straps secured the low-cut bodice in place he had no idea, but it clung to accentuate the generous swell of her breasts and brought him out in a sweat. His mouth went dry. Heart pounding, his pulse raced as his gaze continued down, seeing how the fabric skimmed the gentle flare of her hips and the trousers shaped the lush curve of her rear before moulding the length of her long legs. The creamy colour of the one-piece suit brought out the olive tones of her skin, the fabric covered in silver-grey threads that shimmered as she moved. Conor stared, overcome with heat and arousal. The temptation to touch was unbearable. No way was he going to get through this evening. Smothering a groan, he thrust his hands into his pockets in an attempt to stop himself giving in to his baser instincts. All he wanted was to lock the door, strip off her clothes and spend the whole night lovingly and thoroughly exploring every inch of her.

'Are the kittens all right?'

'The kittens?' He struggled to find his voice and force his mind to focus on something other than anticipating the pleasure of making love with Kate. 'Um, yes, they're fine. They've had a mad run around and a good supper and were asleep when I left.'

His gaze followed as she moved around the room, collecting her things. He couldn't forget how she had felt in his arms, how she had tasted that day in the car park when passion had raged between them. How could she deny what they had? She had been as aroused as him, urgently pulling at his clothes, rubbing herself on him as her body had sought the fulfilment they had both craved. He wanted her so badly it was a physical ache. And now he had to spend the evening with her dressed like that and not touch her? No way was he going to survive this. And no way was any other man laying hands on her. Nic could be trusted for a couple of dances but that was it. Whether she liked it or not, he was staking his claim on Kate and woe betide anyone who tried to move in on his territory tonight.

Kate collected her jacket and bag, checking she had her mobile in case of emergencies, and turned to face Conor, halting at the raw expression in his sultry green eyes. It was hot and sexy and scarily intent. Hell, she had known this outfit was a mistake. Having braved the subject with Aileen and been told several members of the surgery staff would be attending the dinner with their partners, Kate had found herself at the address Hannah had given her and been taken under the wing of Moira Montgomery, the elegant, middle-aged woman who owned the select clothes shop. She had fallen for the shimmery trouser suit the second she had seen it. On the rail it had looked classy but once on her eyes had widened in alarm when she had looked at herself in the mirror.

'I don't think I should wear this,' she had breathed, concerned it was too revealing.

'Nonsense, lovey,' Moira had insisted, fussing around her. 'You look magnificent. It could have been made for you.'

Now every millimetre of her flesh tingled under Conor's inspection. His obvious hunger was exciting yet scary, but she was even more frightened by her own response, the rush of desire she was unable to control. Burning with arousal, she could imagine the whisper of his touch on her skin, the caress of his hands, the taste of his mouth, and her pulse rocketed, her breath lodging in her throat. He looked impressive but unfamiliar in his dark grey suit, white shirt and grey tie. Having disapproved of his style of dress when she had first met him, she now couldn't adjust to him wearing anything else, acknowledging how the casual clothes suited his personality. His hair was semi-tamed but still flopped across his forehead. Her fingers itched to brush it back. What she really wanted to do was rip his clothes off and never leave there tonight at all.

Alarmed at the dangerous electricity sizzling between them, she turned away and fussed with her jacket, thankful when she was covered up.

'Shall we go?' she suggested, her voice crisper than she'd intended as she struggled to hide her reaction and fragile self control.

* * *

Conor found his protective and proprietorial instincts were well to the fore when he escorted Kate out of the flat into the dark evening to the car. He feared the journey would seem a long one and not just because of the wet and windy weather. Initial attempts at conversation, even with safe topics like Lizzie or the kittens, soon fizzled out, which was unsurprising given that the atmosphere between them was charged with tension and desire. Glancing across at her, he noted that her hands were clenched in her lap and, along with his physical hunger, he experienced a deepening need to watch over her. Suddenly troubled, he remembered his conversation with Kyle, his instinct that if and when Kate let go of the pain inside her the fall was going to be a big one. A shiver rippled down his spine and he was alarmed by the inexplicable feeling that something important and life-changing was about to happen. Affected by the charged atmosphere, he flicked on the CD player, hoping the background music would help fill the deafening silence and help them relax. Hands tightening on the wheel, he focused on negotiating the narrow lanes in the difficult conditions, trying to shrug off his unease and push his jumbled thoughts to the back of his mind.

'Hell!' he exclaimed, bringing the car safely to a halt as they rounded a bend to find the road blocked by a serious accident. He turned to Kate, his hand resting on her arm. 'You OK?'

'Fine.'

Her gaze was fixed on the scene and Conor's attention shifted, too, as blue lights from an attending fire engine, ambulance and police car reflected off the wet road in the darkness of the evening.

'I'll see what's going on,' he said, aware Kate was following as he left the car.

It took a moment to make sense of the tangled mess but it appeared a tractor pulling a trailer had crossed the road. A car coming round the bend had seen it too late and the collision had impacted the vehicle under the trailer. Firefighters worked with obvious urgency on the wreckage and Conor could see one paramedic inside the remains of the car. His colleague was running from the ambulance towards the crash site, carrying some equipment.

Recognising the paramedic, Conor joined him. 'What's happening, Ally?'

'Conor. Thank God.' Ally looked stressed and anxious. 'We're in a hell of a mess here, Doc. Ten-year-old boy trapped by his leg in the car. We have fluids up. Airway clear, no head injury. But he's deteriorating fast and he's in shock; his BP is dropping, he's pale and cold. The trapped leg looks non-viable, but we can't access it or the other leg. We fear massive internal bleeding following blunt trauma to his abdomen after the rapid deceleration—could be spleen, liver, bowel, anything. The fire service are working as fast as they can but they can't get him out for some time. And there's a major incident elsewhere taking up much-needed personnel. We have no road assistance or air ambulance coming here sooner than twenty minutes. That's far too long. We need him out. Now. Leg or no leg. But none of us have surgical skills.' Worried hazel eyes stared at him. 'He's going to die if we don't do something in a hurry.'

Before Conor could reply, he heard a moan of distress and turned to see that Kate was just behind him. Her face was deathly pale and, as she swayed, he wrapped an arm around her waist, holding her close, feeling her trembling.

'Kate? What's wrong?'

She didn't appear to hear him. He looked into her eyes, alarmed at the look of stark anguish in them. Ignoring him, she turned to Ally, licking her lips and sucking in a deep breath before could speak, her voice rough and shaky.

'Capillary refill?' she demanded.

Ally shot him a querying glance and Conor nodded, not understanding but going along with any idea she might have to help. 'This is Dr Kate Fisher—she's working with us at Glentown.'

'Very prolonged,' Ally informed her, answering her rapid questions, and Conor listened to the brisk conversation, knowing that if it took six seconds or longer for the skin to turn pink after being pressed, as the blood refilled the capillaries, it was a dangerous sign. As Ally had indicated. 'He's top priority, immediate extraction.'

Which meant they had to get him out and off to hospital without any more delay. Another glance at Kate's face and Conor noticed her unnatural pallor, her lips bloodless. But her eyes had changed, now totally blank of emotion and expression, as if she was shutting everything down inside her. It scared him. He remembered the times she had blanked out before but this was different. Worse.

'I need gloves,' she said as Ally's succinct briefing came to an end, and continued to list things she wanted.

'Kate, I don't think—' Conor began, but she was shrugging away from him, moving to the car as Ally rushed off to get what she had asked for. Anxious, Conor turned to her. 'Kate!'

Before he could stop her she was throwing off her jacket and wriggling inside the car to examine the boy and talk to Dave, the other paramedic. Feeling helpless, Conor stood by the wreckage unable to hear what Kate was saying as the firefighters worked on, trying to cut the tangled metal free and gain access to the trapped boy's legs. Remembering where they were meant to be, he took out his mobile and sent a text to Nic to let him know they were helping at an accident scene and might not make it to the dinner. At least their friends and colleagues wouldn't worry if they didn't show. All the worry was his at the moment. For Kate.

Ally returned, handing the gloves and other things inside to Kate and Dave. 'Any other casualties?' Conor asked as they waited for Kate's next move.

'Tractor driver is in shock—one of the policemen has taken him home,' Ally explained, pointing towards the nearby farmhouse. 'The boy's name is Russ. His father, Bryan, is in the back of the ambulance—shock and minor cuts and bruises.'

Kate's starkly white face appeared at the gap where the twisted car door had been removed, that frighteningly blank look still in her eyes as she asked for ketamine, saline and other items. 'And I need more light in here,' she instructed, unrecognisable as the woman he knew.

When Ally had delivered the things Kate had requested, the fire crew stopped work. Kate calculated dosages and administered the ketamine through the IV to anaesthetise Russ, with Dave responsible for monitoring the oxygen and breathing. Once Russ was under, Conor held the light steady and observed as Kate used a tourniquet above the knee, then flushed the open, traumatic wound site with saline before she set to work.

'Air ambulance less than fifteen minutes,' Ally whispered to Conor.

He nodded, all his attention focused on what was happening in the car. 'Right.'

'Is Kate a surgeon?'

He opened his mouth to say no but closed it again, frowning. Did this explain the gaps in her CV? Maybe this was why she knew Professor Fielding-Smythe so well. Struck dumb, he watched as Kate carried out the impossible procedure with a speed and skill he could only marvel at. She didn't even have the right equipment but she never hesitated, Dave and Ally doing exactly what she told them while he directed the light and watched in awe and confusion. If Kate had the training to attempt what she was doing now, why on earth was she working as a GP locum in their rural Scottish practice?

Fighting down the fear and the nausea, Kate tried to blank everything out and do what needed to be done. She had heard the words 'He'll die if we don't do something in a hurry' and she had known she had to act. No one else here could do it. She could. *If* she could find the courage. Too many people had died already. She couldn't stand by and do nothing, knowing that if she had acted the boy might have had a chance. But she didn't know how to make herself face it either.

Her first sight of Russ's injuries had convinced her that the leg was not viable and, with his internal injuries and deteriorating condition, the seriousness of the situation was indisputable. Russ came out now or he died. He might still die, but this way he had a chance—if she could do it and if the air ambulance arrived on time.

Paralysing fear threatened to overwhelm her and she wanted to leave the car. To run. Again. She closed her eyes. The only way she could do this was to blank everything from her mind, operate, literally, on autopilot, forgetting the past, forgetting Conor.

Lying at an uncomfortable angle inside the wreck, her fingers feeling numb and lifeless, she worked on bones shattered beyond repair, tying off blood vessels, saving nerves and tendons, doing the best she could to preserve muscle and take enough viable skin for the surgeons at the hospital to work with.

When Russ was finally able to be removed from the car with the utmost care, they found his other leg had suffered a more minor open fracture and she welcomed help from Conor, Dave and Ally to treat the leg and maintain the boy's fragile clinical condition.

By the time the air ambulance arrived, complete with an experienced trauma doctor on the crew, Russ was ready to go, critically ill but with a chance of survival he would not have had were he still trapped in the car with time running out. She gave her report to the attending doctor in a monotone, never more relieved to abdicate her care of a patient. While Conor and the others were occupied with the transfer, she slipped away, making it nearly as far as the car before reaction set in. Slumping to her knees on the ground, she was violently ill. Then the shaking started. Images and memories flooded her brain. It was too much. Self-preservation kicked in, something inside her switching off, closing her down.

'Where's Kate?' Conor demanded.

'Don't know, Doc.' Ally frowned. 'I haven't seen her since we began the transfer. She was awesome in there.'

Conor glanced round, unable to find her. Russ was safely installed in the air ambulance *en route* to the specialist help he needed—only alive thanks to Kate's skill and quick thinking. Dave and Ally were clearing up and taking Russ's father, Bryan, to hospital by road, while the firefighters and police were making the scene safe. Taking his leave, he picked up their discarded jackets and went in search of Kate, his heart pounding as his worry increased, his mind buzzing with questions. As he neared the car, he saw her slumped at the side of the road and he ran forward.

'Kate!'

She didn't answer. Kneeling down in front of her on the wet grass, he saw she hadn't even taken her gloves off. She looked bedraggled, streaked with blood, and although her eyes were open, she wasn't seeing or hearing anything. She was horribly pale, her body shaking, and she had a haunted look that scared him. Hating to leave her even for a moment, he eased off her gloves then opened the car, put their things inside and returned with a dry blanket. Wrapping it around her, he drew her into his arms and held her close, rocking her, feeling inadequate because he had no idea what was going on and how to help her.

'Katy?' he whispered, voice choked with emotion. She shivered but didn't respond. He stroked the damp strands of hair back from her face and brushed his lips over her cold, pale cheek. 'I'll take care of you. Everything's going to be OK.'

He hoped to God that was true. Rising to his feet, he lifted her into his arms and carried her to the car, gently setting her on the passenger seat and wrapping the blanket around her before securing the seat belt. The drive to his house seemed to take for ever. Kate never stirred, just sat staring into the darkness, deep in one of her trance-like states. When they pulled up at the house, he left her in the car while he opened the front door and turned on the lights, then he went back for her, carrying her inside and up to his bedroom.

'Can you stand for me?' he asked, setting her on her feet in the *en suite* bathroom, holding onto her as she swayed. 'We need to get you cleaned up and warm.'

Her beautiful trouser suit was ruined—wet, dirty, torn and covered in blood. Concerned for her physical well-being and emotional state, knowing she wasn't fit to do anything for herself, he hid his own emotions and began gently stripping off her ruined clothes. She stood like a child while he helped her, his fingers unsteady as he slipped off her shoes and then moved to find and struggle with the side fastening of her one-piece outfit. He soon discovered why the fabric clung to her like a sheer glove—she was wearing virtually nothing underneath it.

This was going to kill him. No matter how much he told himself he was a doctor, that he had to do this for Kate's sake, that it wasn't personal, it was impossible to ignore his feelings. She was so incredibly beautiful.

Don't look! He repeated the words over and over like a mantra in his head. Close your eyes, he told himself. It didn't help. Not one bit. He tossed the garments aside and quickly followed them with his own, keeping his boxers on to maintain some propriety—not that Kate was in a fit state to care.

The most important thing was to get her warmed up and as it didn't seem likely that she could stand safely on her own in the shower, much less wash herself, he needed to get in there with her. Maintaining as safe a distance between their bodies as he could, he drew her under the water, keeping his touch as impersonal as possible as he cleaned her, avoiding the most dangerous no-go areas. A frown creased his brow as he noticed a scar on her left side halfway between her hip and her lower rib, wondering what had caused it, remembering how she had held herself there, passing it off as a stitch, the day they had walked up to the Grey Man. In the circumstances he couldn't look closely but from what he could see the wound wasn't very old and hadn't been professionally tended to when fresh. More unanswered questions jostled in his head. Frowning, he rinsed her hair with care then snapped off the shower. He wrapped a towel around her head then reached for another large fluffy one to encase her body before stripping off his wet boxers and knotting a towel around himself.

As she seemed more steady on her feet, he slowly walked her to the bedroom and sat her on the bed, drying her and swapping the towel for a large T-shirt before turning his attention to her hair, combing it through and drying it. When he finally tucked her into his bed, she lay on her back, staring up at the ceiling, her hands shaking as they clutched the duvet. He was loath to give her any medication until he had a better idea what was wrong. Her pulse and her breathing were normal. This was something deeply emotional, part of the cracking process he so feared might happen if she didn't release whatever inner pressure she was carrying. And she still hadn't cried, was keeping everything buried inside her. He knew a little more now, at least in terms of the professional skills she had hidden, but not enough for any of the jigsaw pieces to fit and the picture to make sense. For a while he sat in silence, stroking her hair until she seemed to settle, some of the tension leaving her body, her hands relaxing their death-like grip on the duvet.

'Kate, can you hear me?' An imperceptible nod was his only answer, but at least a response was there, a sign she was emerging from the dark, lonely place in which she had shut herself. 'Would you like a drink?' Again the tiny nod. But his suggestion of water brought a negative shake. 'Hot chocolate?' This time the nod was firmer. 'Just rest. I'll be back in a couple of minutes, I promise.'

Conor hated leaving her. Covered only with the towel around his waist, he hurried downstairs, locking up his car and the house before going to the kitchen. The kittens were fine, stirring while he made the hot chocolate then settling back in their beds. He laced her drink with a splash of brandy before carrying the mug upstairs and setting it on the side cabinet. Kate hadn't moved but she seemed less rigid and un-focused. Taking a chance, he slid into bed beside her, helping her sit up before handing her the mug. As she cradled it in trembling hands, he drew her into his arms, holding her as she slowly sipped her drink, the aroma of the chocolate mingling with the citrusy fragrance of her hair and skin.

When she had finished, he took the empty mug from her and set it aside, surprised but delighted when she snuggled closer rather than pulling away, as he had feared she would. There were so many things he needed to know but he held his tongue, rocking her gently, one hand stroking her hair as she relaxed more against him. He closed his eyes, only to open them again as all he could see in his mind was Kate—not just her beauty and how she had looked and felt, but he would never forget the terrible pain and stark trauma in her eyes back at the accident site.

Kate allowed herself to rest in the comforting circle of Conor's arms, reality and memory returning, having shut down after the horror had become too much to bear. She had done what had needed to be done but it had taken everything out of her, brought back all her nightmares, and she could never have moved, never have functioned if Conor hadn't taken over.

Embarrassment churned inside her at how helpless she had been, how many liberties she had granted him. And now she was in his bed, wearing nothing but a T-shirt that carried the lingering earthy scent of him. She couldn't believe she had allowed him to undress her, wash her, care for her. He'd been amazing, though, not pressing her for answers to the questions he must have, caring for her with a gentle kindness and compassion that made her want to weep. But she couldn't cry. Even now. If she did, she would never stop.

As her senses reawakened, she became more aware of Conor's presence, the safety she felt in his arms, the warmth and scent of his body, the feel of his bare chest beneath her cheek—warm skin, rippling muscle, the dusting of hair. The temptation to turn her head and press her mouth to his flesh was overpowering. Despite her efforts to keep him at a distance, her body gravitated to his and she curled into him, seeking comfort, lulled and aroused at the same time. As she fought to keep the memories at bay, she knew she would have to leave Glentown, that her haven of calm was over. There would be questions, interest, intrusions she couldn't cope with. The thought of leaving this place and these people, especially Conor, was painful, but her nightmares were worse, driving her on, keeping her moving because she wasn't strong enough to confront them.

She snuggled closer. For tonight she could banish everything from her mind. It was wrong but for these few hours she could take what Conor offered, what she needed so badly. Just one night. Then she would have to go—to find somewhere else where she could start over, make fresh decisions about what she was going to do with her life, whether she could even carry on being a doctor if she was going to go to pieces every time something like this happened.

'Do you want to talk?'

Conor's words, husky and soft, drew her from her thoughts and she shook her head. 'No,' she murmured, feeling the thud of his heart, knowing her own pulse was speeding up at what she was thinking and doing, her breath catching in her chest.

'Maybe you should sleep now,' he suggested, his voice unsteady.

'No.' She turned into him, looking into his darkening green eyes. 'Stay with me.'

She felt him tense, heard the longing underlying his words. 'You don't know what you're asking.'

'I do.' Her hand moved, her fingertips exploring his chest.

'Not now,' he said, catching her hand in his. 'I don't want to take advantage of this.'

Ignoring his protest, she wriggled closer, pressing her mouth to the strong column of his throat, loving his taste. 'Please, Conor, make me forget.'

'Tonight?'

'Everything.' She leaned in, nibbling along his bottom lip, hearing his breath catch. 'Just for a while, make it all go away.'

'Kate, don't,' he groaned.

'I need this…need you.'

'Kate…'

Conor struggled to maintain his willpower. It was torture to hold back but he didn't want to abuse her trust. She'd been distressed, she was… Dear heaven! Kate's tongue teased the outline of his mouth. His hands moved to her sides to keep some distance between them but they tightened as her fingers returned to their exploration of his chest, his heart pounding as they brushed around and across a sensitive nipple. She smiled against his mouth at his involuntary response.

'Please, Conor.'

As if he could deny her anything. As if he didn't want her like a crazy person. Any chance he had of being honourable evaporated as she kissed him, teasing forgotten, and his mouth opened hotly under hers, swallowing her whimpers of encouragement. She wriggled on top of him, pressing her body against his, setting him on fire. Her T-shirt rode up so he felt peachy-soft skin under his hands. He was a flesh-and-blood man, not a bloody saint. A man pushed beyond the limit of his endurance. Wresting control from her, he rolled them over until she was beneath him, welcoming the feel of her hands on his skin. Passion flared in an instant. The kiss deepened, hot and demanding, her tongue twining with his, her fingers urgent as they roamed his body. He shuddered as she dragged her nails down his spine. Her touch, her taste, her fragrance drove him insane but he wanted more. Much more. Wrenching his mouth free, he looked into sensual brown eyes, hands unsteady as he drew off the T-shirt, tossing it aside.

'Katy,' he whispered. 'You're so beautiful.'

She gasped, her body arching to him as his fingers traced the outline of her breasts, seeing the flush of arousal on her skin, dusky-rose nipples peaking in anticipation of his touch. Her hands pulled at him but he took his time, savouring her as he had longed to do, smiling at her impatience as his fingertips spiralled slowly inwards to where she most craved them. She cried out when he reached his goal, so responsive to him. One hand sank into his hair, urging his mouth down, and he gave her what she needed, what they both needed, circling her areola with his tongue tip before opening his mouth on her flesh and hungrily drawing the swollen nipple deep inside, drunk on the taste of her, the feel of her.

'Conor!'

'Is that good?' he mouthed against her skin.

She writhed beneath him, struggling to get closer. 'Yes! More…please,' she whimpered.

He could do this for hours; would never get enough of her. He turned his attention to her other breast as her hands grazed urgently down his back and struggled to free the towel. Moving to help her, he groaned as she pulled it free and there was nothing more between them, feeling her heat as she shifted to bring them intimately into contact. If he wasn't careful this was going to be over in five minutes and he didn't want that. He slid lower, taking his time kissing and caressing his way down to her navel, finding her just as sensitive and responsive there, her body squirming to his as he licked, nibbled and sucked on her skin.

Kate whimpered as his fingers found the scar on her side, her body tensing as his lips whispered across the wound. Her hands fisted in his hair and he looked up, seeing the denial in her eyes.

'Don't.'

'What happened?'

She shook her head and he allowed her to distract him. Deliciously. 'No more waiting,' she urged, her hands gliding down, driving him to the edge of reason.

Aroused beyond bearing, he gave in. Later, he promised himself. Later there would be time to love her for hours as he yearned to, to ask all his questions. Reaching out, he dragged open the bedside drawer, scrabbling inside.

'Pray there are some condoms in here,' he told her hoarsely, unable to remember how long ago it had been since he'd needed them. 'And that they're not past their use-by date.'

Impatient, wanting Conor with a desperation she had never experienced before, Kate moaned with frustration. 'Hurry,' she begged, unable to hold on much longer.

Relieved when he found what he was looking for, she took it from him, looking into his eyes as she rolled it on, fingers lingering, feeling his response, welcoming his weight as she drew him down, mouths meeting hotly. She wanted this, needed it. Her body had known from the first; for tonight her head ceased arguing and putting obstacles in the way.

'You're sure?' Conor's voice was rough with tension, green eyes dark with passion.

'Yes.' Her hands moved down to encourage him, gasping as he moved into her and smoothly united them. 'Yes!'

'Katy,' he groaned, one arm sliding under her hips, his free hand sinking in her hair.

She wrapped her legs around him, demanding everything, giving everything. Nothing had ever been like this. The terrible burning inside her threatened to consume her and only Conor could ease the ache, extinguish the fire. She couldn't stand it. Moving with him, desperate for release, she clung on to him, burying her face in his shoulder, sobbing as he took her higher and higher. For what felt like an eternity she teetered on the precipice, balancing on the edge of an unimaginable abyss, until Conor, at last, allowed her to plummet over the edge, his hold tightening, keeping her safe, as they fell together into the most intense, impossible explosion of pleasure, beyond anything she had ever imagined. Incredible. Frightening. Wonderful. They collapsed together, hearts pounding, breathing laboured, bodies entwined. Kate closed her eyes, surrendering to the magic of this night with Conor, knowing she could never repeat it.

CHAPTER ELEVEN

CONOR struggled awake, bitter disappointment surging through him when he discovered he was alone. Frowning, concerned for Kate and worried about the future, he hugged her pillow, drawing in her lingering scent, an ache of longing leaving a hollow loss inside him. Closing his eyes, he relived the most amazing night of his life. Kate was incredible; uninhibited, intensely sensual. Their passion had been hot and insatiable. After the first urgent coming together, they had spent hours learning each other; he had loved every inch of her, while her hands and her mouth had brought him to the edge time and again. Rather than feeling sated, he yearned for more. More of Kate. For ever wouldn't be long enough. But she had gone.

His mobile phone beeped with an incoming text and he was both relieved and annoyed to discover it was from Kate.

I'm at the flat. I'm fine. I need time alone. Please. K.

Shit!

Conor didn't believe for one second she was fine. Cursing, he slid from the bed, anxious about her emotional and physical state. Scared that she was backing off again, he went to shower, his heart clenching as he found her ruined outfit on the floor. The last thing Kate needed to be was on her own. He tipped his face to the water, angry with himself for giving in to temptation last night. Yes, he'd wanted her, but he had known there were unresolved issues and he had been frightened she had been reacting to circumstances and would regret it. Too late he knew he had been right. He had to be with her, knew his own feelings, but Kate kept pushing him away and he was scared he was being a fool, that he was opening himself up to heartbreak.

Back in the bedroom he sat on the bed, frowning over what to do. He wanted to go round there straight away but was worried he would make things worse if he pushed her. Whatever had affected her so deeply at the accident site—and the times she had blanked out before—was important and bad and buried inside her. Hiding her surgical skills lay at the root of her inner torment. Had some procedure gone wrong? Did she blame herself? There was so much he needed to know, but reacting the wrong way now could ruin everything. But he couldn't do nothing. Full of uncertainty, he reached for his mobile and composed a text of his own.

Kate, I'm worried about you. I'll give you space today if that's what you want but I'm always here for you if you need anything at all. Please call me. Any time. Love, Cx.

They needed to talk. Most of all Kate needed to release whatever was causing her so much pain. How much did Fred know? Anxious not to leave the house in case Kate returned or called him, he paced away the day, worrying and thinking, even the antics and company of Smoky and Willow failing to cheer him. He spoke briefly to Kyle and to Nic about what had happened, his anxieties over Kate and his feelings, then phoned Fred to give him basic details of the accident the previous evening, hearing his partner's genuine distress.

'Did you know Kate has surgical skills?' he asked, trying to keep any accusation and resentment from his tone.

'I knew she had done some training on James's team; he said she could have been a good surgeon but her heart was in general practice. She had some crisis of confidence, through no fault of her own, but I don't know more than that, Conor. Truly. How is she?' the older man added after a short pause, concern in his voice.

'Not good.'

'You've fallen for her, haven't you?'

Conor closed his eyes, feeling as if his heart was cracking. 'Yes, Fred, I have. And I'm going to do everything I can to help her. Can we shelter her from this at the surgery?'

'Of course. There's bound to be interest—what Kate did was amazing, especially as everyone believes she is just a normal GP—but I'll speak to all the staff today and make sure no one questions her,' he promised.

'Thanks.'

'What are you going to do?'

He ran a hand through his hair, an idea forming in his mind. 'I'll see how Kate is tomorrow, but I might need a day or two off.'

'No problem, Conor. Whatever you have to do for Kate. Any news of the boy?'

'I rang the hospital. He's come through the operation and is stable but critical in Intensive Care,' Conor replied, knowing Russ only had this chance thanks to Kate's actions.

After a sleepless night Conor arrived at the surgery on Monday morning to find a worried Aileen waiting for him.

'Fred told me yesterday. You look terrible,' she fretted, her grey eyes anxious.

Conor manufactured a wry smile. 'Thanks.'

'We'll look after Kate, pet, don't worry,' Aileen reassured him. 'I'm fielding all calls. We've had a couple of press queries.'

'I was afraid of that. Let's keep Kate out of it if we can. Put anything through to me...or Fred if I'm not here.' His gaze strayed down the corridor. 'Is Kate in yet?'

'She is.'

Nervous tension made him feel sick. 'I need a few minutes to talk to her.'

'Let me know if there's anything I can do to help,' the perceptive woman offered, her smile understanding.

'There is one thing…'

After outlining his plan and gaining Aileen's enthusiastic support, Conor went to Kate's consulting room, taking a deep breath before knocking on the door. He stepped inside, his throat closing as he saw her pallor, the dark circles under her eyes. Her gaze slid from his as she clasped tremulous hands together on her desk. Uncertain, he sat down, wondering how to get through to her.

'No one is going to be bothering you about Saturday,' he began, wishing she would look at him. 'Aileen is monitoring the calls and if there are any questions, Fred or I will deal with them.'

'Thanks.' The word whispered out, husky and raw.

'There are bound to be questions, but we'll do all we can to field them…if that's what you want.'

'Yes.'

'Kate, we need to talk.'

She shook her head, her hair falling to shield her face. 'There's nothing to say.'

'Please, don't do this,' he begged, fear making him edgy.

'It was just a night, Conor,' she insisted, voice shaky. 'I'm sorry. It shouldn't have happened. It didn't mean anything.'

Conor stared in disbelief. This was worse than he'd expected. 'I don't believe that and I don't think you do either. What we have is special, Kate.'

'It can't be.'

The panic in her voice tore at his heart and he rose to his feet, rounding the desk to crouch beside her, taking one cool, trembling hand in his. 'I know you're scared about something. Hurting. Let me help you. Please.'

'You can't,' she insisted, withdrawing her hand from his.

Frustrated, concerned, confused, he wanted to pull her into his arms, hold her, shake her, demand answers, anything to break through her emotional barriers, but he returned to his chair to stop himself doing something dumb. It was time to change tactics and put his plan into action. No matter how Kate tried to deny it, he knew what they had was amazing and he wasn't going to give up until she faced whatever inner torment was keeping them apart. It hurt that she couldn't trust him and he was scared she was going to run, so he had to act now if he hoped to help her and give them any chance for a future together.

'I know this isn't the best time, Kate, but would you do me a favour?'

She glanced at him for the first time, wariness in her eyes. 'What kind of favour?'

'I have to go away for a few days and—'

'You're going away?' she interrupted, with a mix of shock, relief and alarm.

'Not for long.' He couldn't bear the thought of leaving her, even for a short time, but it was essential. 'Would you look after Willow and Smoky for me?'

'Of course.' She frowned, wrong-footed by his request. 'When?'

Conor hid his relief, hoping the kittens would be his insurance policy and that she cared too much to abandon them and run while he was gone. 'I'll bring them and their things over at lunchtime.'

'Right.'

'I'll leave you to get on, then.'

With a supreme effort of will he rose to his feet. Aware she was puzzled and unsettled, he left the room and went in search of Aileen, getting the information he needed before making arrangements with Fred. He was going to fight for Kate Fisher.

Unable to sleep, Kate sat in the dark living room, two sleepy kittens cuddled in her lap. She welcomed their warmth and company. Not for the first time she felt horribly alone but this time it was more cutting, more raw. Conor had gone away. One moment he claimed he cared, the next that he was going on holiday. She cursed her contrariness. She had told him to leave her alone, had said she didn't want him, and that was the best thing for both of them. But she had never expected to feel so bereft. To need him so much. She was so confused. And scared. Making love with Conor had been a stupid mistake. How had she ever thought she could take one night and it wouldn't matter? Making love with Conor had been the most stupendous thing that had ever happened to her, the explosion of hot passion indescribable. Her own behaviour had been out of character: she had responded to him with wild abandon and a complete lack of inhibition. Thinking about the things they had done brought a flush to her face and she pressed cool palms to her cheeks, trying to block out the memory of the unimaginable pleasure she had experienced with him.

Had circumstances been different, she could have settled in her rural Scottish haven, but Saturday night had far-reaching consequences. There would be repercussions, no matter how Conor and her colleagues tried to shelter her. They couldn't protect her from her own nightmares. People would start asking questions, wondering about her, wanting to know how a supposedly ordinary GP had carried out such a surgical procedure. There would be questions about her past. And Conor would have all manner of questions of his own that she couldn't face answering. However painful, she had to leave before the past caught up with her. If only she had never succumbed to temptation in Conor's bed. She had known one night wouldn't be enough but in her weakest moment she had grasped what he had offered, needing to forget everything else. In the process she had opened herself up to more hurt because she had done the most unforgivable thing of all. She had fallen in love with Conor Anderson.

* * *

Unable to book the flights he wanted, Conor opted for the freedom to move where and when he needed and drove. By the time he reached London on Monday night he was physically tired and mentally exhausted. He parked outside the address he had been given and, taking his overnight bag, he walked up the path and rang the front doorbell.

'Welcome, Conor,' his host greeted him, stepping back to let him in. 'I've been expecting you.'

'Thank you.' After shaking hands, Conor followed Kate's father to a cosy sitting room.

'You must be tired and hungry. What can I get you?' Tom offered.

Worried about leaving Kate, Conor ran a hand through his wayward hair. 'I'm sorry it's so late. I don't want to put you out.'

'You're not, believe me. How about a sandwich and a coffee?'

'That sounds great,' he admitted with a weary smile.

'Make yourself at home—there's a cloakroom across the hall,' the older man said. 'I'll be back in a few moments.'

Left alone, he thought of Kate, wondering how she was coping. He scanned the bookshelves along one wall of Tom's sitting room before surveying the rest of the room, noticing the photo frames on the piano. He walked across, his heart lurching as his gaze zeroed in on one of Kate. She looked happy, her eyes bright, revealing none of their current soulful pain, as she snuggled up with an attractive young man. A mix of emotions chased through him: gut-wrenching jealousy; aching hurt for whatever had happened to turn this carefree woman into the one who had arrived in Glentown-on-Firth; a determination that Kate would look like this again, would laugh with him and be free.

'Conor?'

He jumped at the sound of Tom's voice, guiltily setting the photo back on the piano. 'Sorry.'

'Not at all.' Tom's gaze flicked to the photograph then back to him, a knowing smile curving his mouth. 'You're in love with my daughter.'

Conor swallowed. 'I am,' he agreed, relieved when Tom nodded in apparent approval and set down a tray containing a plate of sandwiches and a pot of coffee.

'So,' Tom commented once they were settled, 'I assume something has happened to bring you here in a hurry?'

'Yes. We had an…incident. On Saturday night,' Conor continued, filling Kate's father in on the details of the accident—but not what had happened afterwards between Kate and himself.

Tom's brown eyes, so like Kate's, clouded with concern. 'That will really have spooked her, Conor, and brought back a lot of hurt. She might run.'

'That's my fear.' He paused, trying to collate his thoughts. 'I've known from the first that something was wrong. Aside from the gaps in her CV, one look at her eyes told me she was hurting. I've tried to encourage her to talk but she won't. I want to help her but I don't know her history, what it is that went wrong.'

'I can tell you some of it. The rest I don't know myself because she's refused to talk since she came home,' Tom admitted.

Conor frowned. 'Home from where?'

'With Kate it was always going to be medicine,' Tom explained after a pause. 'Her goal was always general practice but she met Darren and was swayed by his ambition for a while.'

'Darren?' He forced the question, glancing back at the photo on the piano, wondering if he had a name for the face.

'I never liked him. Darren was not right man for Kate. He was on the professor's team, on his way to being a surgeon. James had been impressed with Kate during her initial training and Darren persuaded her to change her career path. At the end of her GP training, she joined the surgery rotation instead of going straight to a GP job as she'd planned. Darren was charming and knew how to get what he wanted. He had grand schemes for a fancy private clinic, was very self-centred and materialistic, but Kate wised up and ended her relationship with Darren.'

'What happened?'

'My daughter has always been traditional at heart; she's focused on her career but she's always wanted a family of her own. She found out Darren had been playing the field around the hospital behind her back, then she discovered him in compromising circumstances with one of her colleagues. That was two years ago.'

So Darren was the doctor Kate had mentioned. 'Kate thinks I'm like him,' he murmured, remembering her distrust and disapproval, her reaction seeing him with Jenny, jumping to the wrong conclusions.

'You're nothing like him, Conor. I'm sure she knows that deep down but is using it as an excuse to maintain some distance.'

'Maybe.' He frowned, unconvinced, groaning inwardly when he recalled how he'd been so worried about putting pressure on her by getting too serious too soon that he'd suggested they have some fun, keep it casual—the very thing bound to put her off. Cursing himself for getting things so wrong, he broke off his troubled thoughts as Tom continued with the story.

'The professor has been a mentor to Kate but he was disappointed when she left his team. She returned to general practice but didn't settle. I wasn't surprised when she decided to join an international aid agency—she always had strong views about injustice. Her first trip to Africa was hard but rewarding—the second was much worse. Wes, always the adventurous one, the risk-taker, was already there. Photojournalism gave him the buzz in the field he sought.'

Puzzled by the turn of the conversation, Conor frowned. 'Wes?'

'Wesley. My son,' Tom informed, gesturing to the photo.

So the guy cuddling Kate was her brother? A surge of relief washed through him.

'Wes often spoke of the terrible need and lack of health care in parts of Africa, and Kate had done her elective there during training, so when this posting came up she took it. She was part of a very small team in a remote area and they had been there for some weeks when there was an uprising. The fighting was terrible. Wes was there, covering it for his news-paper. As next of kin, the aid agency told me Kate's group were stranded, under attack, coping with unimaginable casu-alties, amputations, all sorts. She has never spoken of it.'

Conor felt sick as he listened, sure it was much worse than Tom knew. Kate had kept the real horror inside her. Saturday's accident had made her face it again. No wonder it had tipped her over the edge. He wished he was there with her now, keeping her safe.

'Wes was killed. So was Kate's fellow doctor and untold numbers of civilians and rebels. Kate was injured but she carried on alone, unable to get out. I know from speaking with the agency director that she had to do surgery way beyond her training, that there was no one else to help all those people.' Tom paused, emotion raw in his voice. 'When they finally got to her, she was in bad shape, trau-matized, when they evacuated her home nearly four months ago. For a while she said she couldn't be a doctor any more, would never do surgery again. As she healed physically, the prof persuaded her to have a complete change of scene.'

'So she came to us,' Connor filled in, choked up as he struggled to absorb the enormity of all Kate had been through.

'Yes.' Tom smiled, his expression clearing. 'It's been good for her, Conor. I couldn't believe the change in her when I came up—it was like beginning to have my daughter back again. She's bottled everything up inside, about Wes and Africa. It's not healthy.'

As he lay in bed later, trying to get some sleep before the long drive back to Scotland, Conor's mind refused to shut down. He understood the omissions from her CV, the professor's concern to get her the job, why Kate had been terrified that first day with all the doubts inside her about being a doctor. And losing her brother on top of the other horrors, shutting that grief and trauma inside. He physically hurt at the knowledge of what Kate had endured, her amazing strength and courage. And her pain. So much pain and loss. He couldn't begin to imagine what she had seen and done and lost. He couldn't bear to think of her so alone, so scared. She wouldn't be any more— not if he had his way.

'You have my blessing, Conor, and my gratitude,' Tom said as they parted company on Tuesday morning, shaking hands. 'You're just what Kate needs.'

'I hope so, Tom.'

Setting off later than he had intended, Conor prayed that he could help Kate before it was too late.

'Fred, could I have a moment?' Kate asked after final surgery had finished on Tuesday, nerves tightening inside her as he glanced up from his paperwork and smiled, waving her to a chair.

'Of course, my dear. How are you?'

She lowered her gaze, hating lying to him. 'I'm fine.' Taking a deep breath, she steeled herself to get things over with. 'I'm really sorry to cause any difficulties, but I'm going to have to leave,' she told him, cursing the unsteadiness of her voice.

'Oh, Kate.' The heartfelt compassion in his words was nearly her undoing. 'If this is about Saturday, aren't you being too hasty?'

'No.'

'Have you spoken to James about this?' Fred asked after several moments of uncomfortable silence.

'No,' she repeated, suppressing a shiver when she imagined the professor's reaction. 'Not yet.'

Sighing, Fred ran a hand over his bald pate. 'Why not take a few days off when Conor comes back and think this over more carefully?'

'That wouldn't help.' Not with Conor being part of the problem, even the mention of his name spearing her insides with pain.

'Kate?' Reluctantly, her gaze met his, seeing the kindness and understanding in his blue eyes. 'Aside from the fact that we don't want to lose you, do you really feel things are going to be better anywhere else? We all care about you here—why not stay and let us help you?'

Fearing Fred knew rather more than she had thought, she shook her head. 'I can't. You can't.'

'I'm truly sorry you feel that way.' He shook his head, his eyes sad, and she felt a fresh wave of guilt. Fred, Aileen, everyone had been so kind to her. 'If you change your mind, you only have to say. Otherwise, if you're still sure it's what you want, we'll talk again when Conor comes back.'

'Do you know when that will be? Or where he's gone?'

She bit her lip, cursing herself for asking, her chest tightening when Fred's gaze slid from hers. 'Um, no. No, I don't, not exactly,' he murmured, looking evasive, and Kate suspected he did know but for some reason she didn't understand he had chosen not to tell her.

Leaving the surgery and returning to the flat, seeking solace in the kittens' antics, she wondered how she could have made such a mess of everything. She had come there to get her life back on track but had succeeded in making everything a hundred times worse, not only failing to deal with the issues in her professional life but by falling for the one man she felt she couldn't have.

* * *

Maybe things had worked out for the best time wise, Conor decided as he parked outside the surgery after what had felt an interminable journey. He checked his watch. After nine o'clock. A good thing to catch Kate by surprise and off guard. There was a light on in the bedroom of the flat upstairs and he walked round the side of the old granite building to the door of her flat. He rang the bell, waiting a tense few moments before he heard her light footsteps on the stairs and his pulse rate kicked up.

'Who is it?' she asked, sounding husky.

'Conor.'

'Oh!'

Her surprise and dismay were evident and when he didn't hear the bolt being drawn, he stepped closer. 'Open the door, Kate.'

He didn't actually hear her sigh but he could imagine it. Her reluctance was palpable as the door finally opened. Despite the dark circles under her eyes and her paleness, she looked beautiful, her hair mussed, a sleepy bloom on her face. His gaze skimmed down over the baggy T-shirt that fell halfway down her thighs, then lifted to her face, seeing nervousness, confusion and anxiety in her wary brown eyes.

'Is something wrong?' she asked, one hand settling at her throat as if shielding herself.

'Can I come in?'

'I—'

'Please, Kate.' He remembered the kittens and realised they were a way in. 'How are Smoky and Willow?'

Something shuttered in her eyes. 'Fine. You want to see them now?'

'Please. I've missed my girls,' he told her, holding her gaze, her being the most important of them.

'Of course.'

As she stepped back he moved inside, locking the door

behind him before he followed her up the stairs, looking at her shapely calves and the soft curves of her bare thighs. Upstairs she turned and faced him, crossing her arms defensively across her chest.

'Couldn't this have waited until tomorrow morning?'

'Sorry, no.' He managed a passable attempt at an apologetic smile, deliberately misleading her. 'You go back to bed. I'll see to things.'

'What?'

'I said—'

'I heard what you said,' she riposted with a frown. 'I meant, why?'

'Because you're sleepy and I didn't mean to disturb you. Off you go and get comfy. I won't be long with the kittens.'

She looked grumpy as she stared at him. 'Lock the door behind you when you go.'

Kate stomped back to the bedroom. So much for her early night and the hope she might get some much-needed sleep after the turmoil of the last few days. Stupid of her to think Conor was here to see her. She was so contrary. She'd told the man she wasn't interested in him—what did she expect if she didn't even know her own mind? Bemused and not a little anxious, she wriggled back into bed and drew the duvet up to her chin. Why was Conor there? Was it for Smoky and Willow? And where had he been? Thirty-six hours wasn't much of a holiday. She frowned again, hearing him moving about in the kitchen. What was he doing in there? It shouldn't take that long to pack up the kittens' things and go.

Kate tensed in surprise when Conor appeared in her bedroom, carrying two mugs of hot chocolate, and tried to close her mind to how much she still wanted him. It was impossible. Confused, she watched him, wary and uncertain, wondering what he was going to do next. When he handed her both mugs and then sat down on her bed with his back to her and began to take off his clothes, her eyes widened in shock.

CHAPTER TWELVE

'CONOR!' Kate protested, struggling to avoid spilling the drinks in her agitation.

'Mmm?'

Shoes hit the floor before his jumper was pulled over his head and tossed aside. Her gaze strayed inexorably to his broad back, the warm, smooth flesh and play of muscle whose feel she remembered too well, her traitorous fingers itching to touch, hot colour staining her cheeks as she saw the faint marks her nails had left on his skin. When his hands moved to the waistband of his jeans, panic surged through her and she found her voice.

'What the hell are you doing?'

'What does it look like?' he responded with maddening unconcern, as he shrugged out of his jeans and boxers then drew back the duvet so he could slide in beside her. 'Shift over.'

'Conor, we are *not* doing this.'

They weren't, she promised herself, fighting the shameful weakness of temptation, scared that he only had to touch her and her resolve would crumble to dust. Ignoring her anxiety, he adjusted his pillow, took one of the mugs out of her hands and leaned back to sip his drink. The nerve of the man left her speechless. Bewildered, she concentrated on her own drink as the silence stretched between them, but she was painfully aware of his nearness, of that ever-present shimmer of desire that crackled between them like an electric current. She could almost hear the thunder of her heartbeat in the silence of the room. Why the hell was she sitting there? She should leap out of this bed right now and demand he leave. So why couldn't she move? The seconds ticked by until, drinks finished, Conor set their mugs aside. Her pulse skittered as he slid an arm around her, shifting them until her head was resting against him and his fingers were stroking her hair.

'I've resigned,' she murmured, trying to put some distance between them, even if it wasn't physical.

'Have you?' He sounded insultingly unconcerned at the news. 'Don't worry. We can unresign you tomorrow.'

'Sorry?'

'When you change your mind,' he elaborated.

'Why would I want to change my mind?'

'Because you're happy here.' Pausing a moment, the fingers at her hair moved to caress her neck, making her flesh prickle. His voice dropped, soft yet husky. 'Because it's time to stop running.'

Kate stiffened in his hold. 'I don't know what you mean.'

'Yes, you do.' His fingers maintained their soothing caress, lulling her into a false sense of security. 'Do you want to know where I've been?'

'Not particularly,' she lied, feeling the chuckle rumble inside him, her fingers defying her, unable to resist their own explorations over the warm, supple, hair-brushed skin of his chest.

'I went to London.'

Kate tensed, her fingers stilling. 'Really?' Anxiety curled inside her.

'Mmm.'

'W-why?' Her eyes closed as she tried to shut out what she feared was to come.

'I had a very interesting talk with your father.'

Every particle of her being went rigid with shock and dismay. 'Conor—'

'Shh.' He stilled her protests, his hold tightening as she struggled to draw away from him.

'Why?' she whispered again, a shiver of foreboding rippling through her.

'I needed to understand,' he explained, his fingers resuming their rhythmic caress. 'And you need to talk.'

She shook her head, denying him, denying the emotions that threatened to overwhelm her. 'I can't.'

'Yes, you can. You are the bravest, most courageous person I've ever met, Kate.' His voice rang with sincerity and she was frightened at the sting of tears pricking her eyes, scared she couldn't hold on. 'I can't imagine what it must have been like for you out there but I could never have coped as you did.'

'But I didn't cope,' she interjected, emotion threatening to overwhelm her.

'From what I heard, you held everything together in terrible circumstances until help came.'

The guilt and the helplessness and the fear threatened to well up all over again, her voice rising with self-recrimination. 'There was so much death, so much killing. Such senseless waste. I should have helped more but I hadn't a clue what I was doing. I panicked, Conor. Cool Kate, always so calm in a crisis, wanted to abandon ship, hide, *die*—anything to get out of there. Then I came home and I lost it, running away from everything like a coward because I can't hack it any more.'

'Oh, Katy, that's not true,' he murmured roughly, his arms tightening, his hands comforting. 'Listen to me. You were alone in a terrifying and dangerous situation, trying to do things beyond your training level. You were physically exhausted, wounded, had little help and you were grieving for your brother and your colleagues. You were understandably scared and tired and ill. Yet you still carried on, saving as many lives as you could until help arrived. You did more—unspeakably more—than any one person could ever be expected to do. You are remarkable, Kate, and I'm so proud of you. Anyone would have been overtaken by the enormity of even a fraction of what you went through. It's hardly surprising that reaction set in once it was over and your body just shut down. It was too much. And you still haven't cried, you're still holding it all inside. You have nothing to feel guilty for, you are not to blame. It's time to let go. Time to acknowledge that you did what you could—and that that was truly amazing.'

'No!'

'Yes,' he pressed, refusing her any respite. 'You have to release this burden.'

She shook her head, trying to fight the emotion, to block out his rawly determined words. 'I can't,' she cried, angry at him for pressuring her, panic clawing ever closer.

'Why not?'

'Because I'm scared it won't stop, that I'll never pick myself up again,' she argued, her words catching, her body shaking with the effort of keeping herself together.

Gentle fingers stroked her face as he held her close, his voice husky in her ear. 'I'll always pick you up, Katy.'

'Conor—'

'Let it go. Trust me.'

She felt as if her last handhold had been ripped from her. The ground slipped away beneath her and she was in free fall. Tears started to flow, huge, hot tears coursing down her cheeks. It was like a dam had been breached, all her defences crumbling under the weight of the torrent, and everything came gushing out, all the pent-up pain, guilt, fear and grief. She turned in Conor's arms, burrowing into him as she sobbed out the hurt.

'It's OK,' he soothed, sounding as if he himself was on the point of cracking. 'I'm here. I've got you. I'm not going to let anything happen to you.'

She had no idea how long the storm lasted but Conor held her, keeping her safe, his warmth and strength seeping into her. Almost without conscious thought or free will, she found herself telling him everything, all the things she had never been able to tell anyone else, that she had never come to terms with: the terror of the gunfire and shelling; the noise; the smells; the blood; the suffering; people dying all around her; the mindless cruelty; the loneliness; anger; fear; and always the guilt that she hadn't been good enough.

'I was so scared, so useless,' she sobbed. 'There was so much I couldn't do.'

'But so much you *did* do to help many, many people who would have had nothing had you not been there,' he insisted quietly.

'But what good did I do them, Conor? What kind of life did I give them?' she demanded, wiping furiously at her tears. 'I didn't become a doctor to cut shattered limbs off innocent children.'

'Oh, Kate.' His voice was thick with answering emotion and he wrapped his arms more securely around her, as if trying to absorb her pain.

'Wesley, he—' She snapped off the words, unable to say it.

'He what?'

She shook her head, ashamed of her feelings. 'Nothing.'

'You're angry with him.'

'Sometimes,' she admitted, surprised anew at his perception. 'I miss him so much. He was brave, foolishly so sometimes. I told him not to go after that final story but he wouldn't listen. Everything was an adventure to him.' Fresh emotion welled inside her. 'I'm mad at him for leaving me there, for abandoning me, for not coming back. What does that make me?'

'Human, Kate, like the rest of us.'

She sniffed, taking the umpteenth tissue he had offered her. 'When I got home London seemed too oppressive and mad. Everything that had once been familiar and comfortable was suddenly alien and distressing. I'd lost a bit of weight, felt run down and stressed out.'

'And you had your injury.'

'Yes.' A flush tinged her tear-stained cheeks, a very different kind of shiver rippling through her as his fingers slid under her T-shirt and caressed the scar on her side.

'You didn't take care of yourself,' he chided.

'There was only me, Conor, and medications were so short. Others had far more need of them than I did. It was a flesh wound—the bullet missed anything vital.'

She felt a tremor run through him as she talked about her injury. 'It became infected?' he asked with obvious concern.

'Yes. But I'm fine now,' she murmured, distracted by the feel of his touch on her skin.

'I can understand why you wanted to shield your dad from all this, especially as he was grieving for Wesley, too, but wasn't there a friend, anyone, you could talk to?'

'Most people can't understand or don't want to. They prefer not to acknowledge how bad things are in other parts of the world, they don't want it to upset their cosy lives. Either they see what aid workers do as crazy or they think we are some kind of heroes, and neither is true. People volunteer for many different reasons.' She frowned, feeling exhausted as she rested against him. 'There just seemed a distance between me and the people I'd known before. I'd been away nearly a year by then, our lives were so different, we didn't connect any more.'

Held safe in his arms in the darkness of the night, she expunged the pain, exorcised the ghosts. And something she had never expected began to happen. A new calmness and sense of peace slowly began to ease the maelstrom of torment inside her, as if everything that had been eating away at her had been washed away. She felt almost ill from the crying that had ravaged her but there was a sense of release, of things shifting back into balance.

'Do you want to go back?' Conor asked after a while.

'Not to aid work.' She welcomed the way he linked the fingers of one hand with hers, giving her strength. 'I've done my bit. I couldn't live that life any more. But I think I'd like to go back to Africa one day. Make some new memories. Some better ones.'

His free hand returned to stroke her hair, his fingertips caressing her neck. 'What about your career?'

'I wondered for a time if I could still be a doctor.'

'And now?'

She sighed, trying to organise her jumbled thoughts—not easy the way her body responded to his touch. 'I can't face surgery any more but being a GP…I've enjoyed it.'

'You're an amazing doctor, Kate.' A warm glow burned inside her at his words. 'Russ is holding his own. He's going to have a long recovery, but he's alive thanks to you. His parents want to meet you and thank you. And all your patients love you—you've given the people here so much.'

'They're easy to care about.'

'So why don't you stay?'

It was tempting but she couldn't see him every day and not be more to him than a practice partner. Neither could she watch him with other women. 'I don't think so.'

'I want you here, Kate.' He sounded so serious, so sincere that she lifted her head from his chest, her teary gaze drawn to his. The emotion in the green depths amazed her. 'With me. Please.'

'W-with you?' she said in a shocked whisper.

A wry smile curved his mouth. 'Is the idea so terrible?' he teased, failing to mask the edge of anxiety.

'It's not that, but…' Her words trailed off as she struggled to voice her concerns. 'You want a quick fling—'

'Do I?'

'Don't you?'

'No.' He released her hand, his fingers lifting to brush the lingering wetness from her cheeks. 'What do you want?'

Everything, the whole happy ending, but it wasn't going to happen. She tried to move away because being so close to him made it impossible to think straight, but his hold tightened, keeping her close. 'It doesn't matter.'

'It does to me.'

'It wouldn't work, Conor, we're too different. You flit from woman to woman. You're phobic about commitment and—'

'You think I don't want commitment?' he interrupted.

Kate frowned in confusion at the surprise and challenge in his voice. 'Do you?'

'I want you to be a partner in the practice, if that's what you'd like, but most of all I need you in my life,' he insisted, his lips whispering against her skin. 'I love you, Kate. More than anything I want to settle down with you and have a family.'

Tears stung her eyes and she shook her head, trying to take it in. This wasn't what she'd expected, but he sounded genuine. 'Why haven't you, then? Settled down, I mean.'

'All I remember from my childhood is my parents' terrible marriage, the vindictive divorce and the stream of failed relationships and marriages that followed for both of them. I've lost count of the number of times my mother has married, the trail of devastation left in her wake.' His thumb brushed her cheek as he continued. 'I vowed that would never happen to me, that I wouldn't make those mistakes. I want it to be right, Kate. I don't want to put any child through the kind of thing I faced.'

Kate struggled to concentrate. 'But I thought—'

'You thought I was another Darren,' he chided.

'But all the women.'

'Just because I went on dates and have women friends doesn't mean I sleep with them, or even kiss them, for that matter. I've been much more choosy than you give me credit for. Why do you think I was in such a panic on Saturday night that the condoms might have been past their use-by date?'

The very thought of that night made her blush. She

frowned, thinking back, realising she had been so desperate for him that his scramble for the box in the drawer hadn't really registered. Could it really be true that he loved her? She hardly dared to believe it.

'But you said you just wanted some fun while I was here,' she reminded him, seeing him wince.

'A stupid misjudgement on my part.' He smiled, brushing some wayward strands of hair back from her face. 'You were so wary, so skittish, I thought you'd freak if I told you how serious I was and I'd frighten you away, so I planned to take it slowly, keep it casual. I didn't know that was exactly the wrong thing to do after what you had been through.'

'I don't understand.'

He smiled patiently at her frown. 'I knew from the first second I saw you that I was going to marry you.'

'W-what?' She stared at him, open-mouthed in shock, her heart thudding uncontrollably. 'But you don't even know me.'

'Don't be silly, Kate,' he chastised with a gentle smile. 'You're the other part of me that makes me feel whole and complete for the first time in my life.'

Kate swallowed, sure she was going to cry again. 'I am?'

'Convincing you has been another matter entirely.' The fingers of one hand slid back under her T-shirt, tracing distracting circles on her skin. 'I thought you'd say I was crazy if I dropped to my knees that first morning and begged you to marry me. You were so beautiful, so sad, so scared. I love you, Kate. All of you. Everything about you. Your compassion and ability as a doctor, your goodness as a person, your courage, your humour, your intelligence. As for what you do to me…' He drew her hand to his chest and she felt the rapid thud of his heart under her palm. 'I've never felt anything like this before. You turn my insides to mush. Kissing you, touching you, making love with you—nothing has ever been like this, Kate. I want to spend the rest of my life with you, loving you.'

'Oh, Conor.' The words escaped as a half laugh, half sob, her mind clearing, her fears fading. She couldn't doubt Conor's sincerity, could no longer deny her feelings for him, the amazing chemistry and bond between them. 'I love you, too.'

Overwhelmed with relief and happiness, Conor sank a hand into Kate's silken hair and drew her head down for a kiss, sighing with contentment as her mouth opened on his, hot and demanding, and the hungry desire flared out of control in an instant, just as it always did. She whimpered, pressing her body against his, her fingers gliding over his skin. There was only one place this was going but while he had a fragment of sense left he needed to know something. Rolling them over, he pinned her under him, catching her hands and linking his fingers with hers, smiling as she looked up at him through sultry brown eyes.

'What?' she demanded impatiently, wriggling under him, arousing him beyond bearing.

'Wait a minute.' He gave her more of his weight, keeping her still. 'Will you marry me?'

Disbelief vied with happiness as she looked up at him. 'Yes!'

'And we'll have dozens of babies?'

'I don't know about dozens.' She laughed through her tears. 'But definitely some.'

He had been scared about what would happen when Kate's fall hit her, had never imagined the secrets and the pain she had held inside her had been so traumatic. His heart had nearly broken at her anguish but they were through the worst now. It would take time but they would face it together and could look towards a brighter future. Peeling off her T-shirt, he lost himself in the magic of making love with Kate and, when they were finally joined together as one again, Kate wrapping around him, he gave thanks to whatever fates had brought this special woman into his life.

EPILOGUE

ONE late summer evening Kate stood on the roof terrace outside the bedroom, looking at the view.

Their wedding a few weeks ago had been the most special day of her life, her new community and all the practice staff having turned out in force to celebrate the marriage of two of their doctors. Her father had enjoyed every moment, his friendship with Aileen flourishing, and he was visiting often, talking about retiring to the village in the near future. Fred was ecstatic, taking more time to relax and cut back his hours, content that the Solway Medical Centre was in good hands. James, who had flown up with his wife for the weekend, had told everyone who would listen that he was responsible for bringing the happy couple together. Charlie had waited outside the church, Ben devotedly at his heels, while Lizzie Dalglish had been pushed up from the residential home in her wheelchair, grinning her delight as she sat beside Andrea Milne in pride of place. Louise Kerr, gaining in self-esteem as her health improved, had joined them, while Jenny and Mark had rushed back from their own honeymoon to celebrate. Nic and Hannah had been there and Kyle, still recovering from his own problems, had stood up as Conor's best man. There hadn't been a dry eye in Glentown.

Kate smiled, leaning on the railing as her thoughts turned

to their honeymoon. They had gone to Africa, visiting the country she had worked in on her last aid agency assignment, meeting former local colleagues and some of the people she had treated, including children she had felt so guilty about but who were facing their futures with amazing fortitude and thankfulness. There had been moments of sadness for Wesley and colleagues lost, but the trip had allowed her to put things in perspective, to balance bad memories with good ones. After that first week spent facing her past, Conor had surprised her with a special three-night visit to the incredible Ngorongoro Crater in Tanzania, which had been an unforgettable experience. Then they had spent four days in Kenya, where they had visited the Sheldrick elephant nursery in Nairobi. Kate laughed. Only Hannah and Nic would give someone a orphaned elephant as a wedding present! They had some wonderful photographs to show their friends that evening of their fostered baby elephant enjoying her daily mudbath.

Kate felt a deep peace and happiness she had never imagined she could know. She loved her work, her home, her community. She loved Smoky and Willow, who caused havoc wherever they went. Most of all she loved Conor. With every fibre of her being. Sensing his approach behind her, she leaned back against him as his arms enclosed her.

His lips nuzzled the sensitive spot behind her ear. 'Kate, are you all right?'

'I'm fine.' She smiled to herself, relieved now she knew just how fine.

'You've been distracted since we came home,' he said. 'What's wrong?'

'Nothing. Honestly. Not now.'

'Not now?' She heard the concern in his voice, his arms tightening. 'So there was something?'

'I was worried about my anti-malaria medication.'

'You're not feeling well? Why didn't you tell me?'

A smile curved her mouth as she turned to face him. 'I wanted to be sure. Now I am.'

'Sure of what?' he questioned with a frown.

'That everything was all right with the timing being so dodgy.'

Conor's frown deepened, his hands cupping her rear and pulling her closer. 'You're talking in riddles. What timing?'

'You know the dangers of the prophylactic drugs for some people.' She couldn't help teasing him a moment longer, hot desire flaring inside her at his touch. 'Pregnant people.'

Conor stilled, one hand moving round to curve protectively over her belly, a suspicion of moisture filming his green eyes as he stared at her in joyful anticipation. 'You're serious?'

'I am.'

'We're going to have a baby?'

'We are!' His urgent, excited kiss took her breath away. 'Hannah and Nic are coming to dinner!' Kate protested, laughing when he whisked her inside and began stripping off her clothes, her fingers sinking into the thickness of his dark blond hair as he dropped to his knees and pressed his mouth to her navel.

'They'll understand. I intend to celebrate baby number one first,' he murmured, his breath warm against her skin. 'I wonder how it happened.'

'You need me to explain the facts of life, Dr Anderson?' She laughed at his expression.

'It must have been that day you got so wild and the condom broke!' he teased, and a tide of colour warmed her face. 'I can't believe you can still blush! Not after the sinful, shameless things you do to me!'

'Conor!'

Laughing, he tipped her onto the bed, shed his own clothes and followed her down. 'You've made my life so special and happy.'

'I aim to please.'

'Oh, you more than please, sweetheart!'

His suggestive chuckle set her pulse racing, her fingers tightening on his shoulders as he set his mouth to the hollow of her throat. 'You're not too bad yourself.'

'Yeah?'

'Yeah.' She slid her hands down his back and wriggled provocatively under him, smiling at the evidence of his arousal.

'Now you've done it,' he groaned.

'I do hope so!'

For a moment he paused and raised his head, the look in his sexy green eyes warming her from the inside out. 'I love you, Katy. My perfect partner in every way.'

'I love you, too.'

And then they no longer needed words, their bodies taking over and demonstrating the intensity of their feelings and the loving bond between them that grew more special with every passing day. The events of the past had led her to Conor, who had helped her to heal. The past would always be with her, she would never forget, but thanks to Conor she had faced her demons… He had taken all the broken pieces of her life, her very self, and had put her back together, making her whole again. Out of pain and loss had come hope and love…a love now growing new life inside her and cementing the promise of a long and happy future together.

FREE!

4 Books
and a surprise gift!

We would like to take this opportunity to thank you for reading this Mills & Boon® book by offering you the chance to take FOUR more specially selected titles from the Medical Romance™ series absolutely FREE! We're also making this offer to introduce you to the benefits of the Mills & Boon® Reader Service™—

- ★ **FREE home delivery**
- ★ **FREE gifts and competitions**
- ★ **FREE monthly Newsletter**
- ★ **Exclusive Reader Service offers**
- ★ **Books available before they're in the shops**

Accepting these FREE books and gift places you under no obligation to buy. you may cancel at any time, even after receiving your free shipment. Simply complete your details below and return the entire page to the address below. You don't even need a stamp!

YES! Please send me 4 free Medical Romance books and a surprise gift. I understand that unless you hear from me. I will receive 6 superb new titles every month for just £2.89 each, postage and packing free. I am under no obligation to purchase any books and may cancel my subscription at any time. The free books and gift will be mine to keep in any case.

M7ZEF

Ms/Mrs/Miss/Mr ....Initials...
BLOCK CAPITALS PLEASE
Surname ....
Address..

....
....Postcode ....

Send this whole page to:
UK: FREEPOST CN81, Croydon, CR9 3WZ